LOKI: THE MISCHIEF BEHIND THE LEGEND

LOKI: THE MISCHIEF BEHIND THE LEGEND

NORSE MYTHS FROM THE CHILDREN OF ODIN

PADRAIC COLUM

FOREWORD BY
PETER DAVID

EDITED BY
AMY MICHELLE CARPENTER

EBook ISBN: 978-1-68057-354-1
Trade Paperback ISBN: 978-1-68057-353-4
Hardcover ISBN: 978-1-68057-355-8
Cover design by Elona Bezooshko
Cover artwork image by Elona Bezooshko | Psych Digital Ink and Motion

Published by WordFire Press, LLC
PO Box 1840
Monument CO 80132
Kevin J. Anderson & Rebecca Moesta, Publishers
WordFire Press Edition 2022
Printed in the USA
Join our WordFire Press Readers Group for new projects, and giveaways.
Sign up at wordfirepress.com

CONTENTS

FOREWORD
PETER DAVID

Who was Loki?

That's a very good question, and the answer is not an easy one because his background comes from a variety of sources. He is most certainly not entirely of Asgardian blood, his father either being a giant (ancient Norse legends) or a frost giant (Marvel Comics.). Stan Lee pegged him as simply the god of evil, the opposite number of his adopted brother, Thor, determined to do horrible things because, well, everyone knew he was the god of evil, so what point was there in disputing it?

But the truth (if such a word can be used to describe a legendary figure) is a bit more complicated than that. There's no denying that in his original incarnation, Loki was a trickster god, a personality so powerful and entertaining that pretty much every mythos, every religion, has one in their mix. Native Americans call him Coyote. Egyptians called him Set, the Celts called him Puck. In modern time, Bugs Bunny fits the bill, although he actually never originates trouble. He just simply strikes back at someone who gives him grief. Hell, my grandmother used the term *kochleffel:* Literally a soup spoon, but more broadly, someone who loves to stir up trouble.

Loki is an inveterate *kochleffel*, always causing problems. Whether he is cutting off Sif's hair (an act which was alluded to in the "Loki" miniseries streaming on Disney plus) or arranging matters where the ultra-manly Thor has to dress in drag, pretending to be an Asgardian maiden in order to retrieve his beloved hammer, Mjolnir, Loki loves making trouble. He is referred to as sometimes good, sometimes evil, and notoriously difficult to pin down. Sometimes he is an ally, sometimes he is making things happen because, well, he's bored with what he views as the pretentious, vain-glorious oafs who reign over Asgard and sees no harm in trying to take them down a peg or two. He probably figures that it serves them right, that their pretentiousness and beliefs that they are far superior to everyone almost requires some lessons in humbleness to be visited upon them, and who's to say he isn't right.

The real problems come to the fore, however, when Loki—for no damned good reason whatsoever—decides to eat the heart of a deceased witch, Gulveig, whose entire body was consumed by her funeral pyre with the exception of her heart. You'd think that if even fire wants nothing to do with a body part, that would be enough of a warning to steer clear of it. But no, Loki—why we've no idea—takes it upon himself to consume the literally damned thing, and it is from that point on that his nature goes due south. No longer is he merely a trickster. The now thoroughly evil demigod decides to start producing children with a witch named Angerboda. Anyone who has "anger" in their name simply can't be any good, and sure enough, he produces three children who are decidedly outside of the norm: the Fenrir (sometimes Fenris) wolf, the beast that would be called the Midgard serpent, and Hela, the half-human/half-corpse who would become known as the queen of death. He also engineered the death of Baldur the Beloved, an action for which he winds up being tied down in a cave with a serpent hanging over his head, dripping venom onto him. His surprisingly faithful wife, Sigyn, who apparently forgives him for cheating on her with a witch, remains to catch the venom in a cup. But every time she empties it out, the poison burns him, and his struggles cause earthquakes. (Which is really as good an explanation as any, one supposes.). Eventually he is able to slip his bonds and join in the fun of Ragnarok, where his enemies are now brought down for all time.

There is no denying his versatility as a character, much of which has been shaped for modern audiences by the character as he is presented in Marvel films, portrayed by Tom Hiddleston. This Loki has become so popular that when Hiddleston appeared in full costume and makeup at the San Diego Comic Con, the several thousand people in the audience went out of their minds with joy. He could have ordered them to overrun the DC booth and they'd likely have done it. No matter how many times the character gets killed off, he keeps coming back. Even Thanos couldn't dispose of him permanently, and he had the damned Infinity Gauntlet.

The bottom line is that we live in a time where we see our leaders full of themselves, sitting high on thrones built of their own pretensions, and we love the idea of taking them down a few levels. Seeing them brought down to the kind of status that we ourselves have to endure on a daily basis. We know when we watch a presidential debate that if they were asked how much a gallon of milk costs, they would stand there with stupid (well, stupider) expressions on their faces and have no response. Imagine Loki moderating, or even participating in, a presidential debate. Imagine him writing Op-Ed pieces. Imagine him on the Supreme Court. The mind boggles with possibilities as to what sort of damage a trickster god could accomplish in our world, and we would all be the better for it.

Indeed, the film Loki is tremendously sympathetic. He believes himself to be full Asgardian, only discovering halfway through that he is a foundling, the son of frost giants. Until that time he is a faithful son and brother; after that, he wants revenge, and who can blame him? He's been lied to his entire life, and that's a pretty long existence to withhold the truth from him. In these times when those in charge lord it over us with the same absence of care that the Aesir lorded it over humanity, it seems that finally the world has caught up with Loki.

Gods help us all.

—Peter David
Long Island, New York
October 2021

PART ONE
THE DWELLERS IN ASGARD

FAR AWAY AND LONG AGO

Once there was another Sun and another Moon; a different Sun and a different Moon from the ones we see now. Sol was the name of that Sun and Mani was the name of that Moon. But always behind Sol and Mani wolves went, a wolf behind each. The wolves caught on them at last and they devoured Sol and Mani. And then the world was in darkness and cold.

In those times the Gods lived, Odin and Thor, Hödur and Baldur, Tyr and Heimdall, Vidar and Vali, as well as Loki, the doer of good and the doer of evil. And the beautiful Goddesses were living then, Frigga, Freya, Nanna, Iduna, and Sif. But in the days when the Sun and Moon were destroyed the Gods were destroyed too—all the Gods except Baldur who had died before that time, Vidar and Vali, the sons of Odin, and Modi and Magni, the sons of Thor.

At that time, too, there were men and women in the world. But before the Sun and the Moon were devoured and before the Gods were destroyed, terrible things happened in the world. Snow fell on the four corners of the earth and kept on falling for three seasons. Winds came and blew everything away. And the people of the world who had lived on in spite of the snow and the cold and the winds fought each other, brother killing brother, until all the people were destroyed.

Also there was another earth at that time, an earth green and beautiful. But the terrible winds that blew leveled down forests and hills and dwellings. Then fire came and burnt the earth. There was darkness, for the Sun and the Moon were devoured. The Gods had met with their doom. And the time in which all these things happened was called Ragnarök, the Twilight of the Gods.

Then a new Sun and a new Moon appeared and went travelling through the heavens; they were more lovely than Sol and Mani, and no wolves followed behind them in chase. The earth became green and beautiful again, and in a deep forest that the fire had not burnt a woman and a man wakened up. They had been hidden there by Odin and left to sleep during Ragnarök, the Twilight of the Gods.

Lif was the woman's name, and Lifthrasir was the man's. They moved through the world, and their children and their children's children made people for the new earth. And of the Gods were left Vidar and Vali, the sons of Odin, and Modi and Magni, the sons of Thor; on the new earth Vidar and Vali found tablets that the older Gods had written on and had left there for them, tablets telling of all that had happened before Ragnarök, the Twilight of the Gods.

And the people who lived after Ragnarök, the Twilight of the Gods, were not troubled, as the people in the older days were troubled, by the terrible beings who had brought destruction upon the world and upon men and women, and who from the beginning had waged war upon the Gods.

THE BUILDING OF THE WALL

Always there had been war between the Giants and the Gods—between the Giants who would have destroyed the world and the race of men, and the Gods who would have protected the race of men and would have made the world more beautiful.

There are many stories to be told about the Gods, but the first one that should be told to you is the one about the building of their City.

The Gods had made their way up to the top of a high mountain and there they decided to build a great City for themselves that the Giants could never overthrow. The City they would call "Asgard," which means the Place of the Gods. They would build it on a beautiful plain that was on the top of that high mountain. And they wanted to raise round their City the highest and strongest wall that had ever been built.

Now one day when they were beginning to build their halls and their palaces a strange being came to them. Odin, the Father of the Gods, went and spoke to him. "What dost thou want on the Mountain of the Gods?" he asked the Stranger.

"I know what is in the mind of the Gods," the Stranger said. "They would build a City here. I cannot build palaces, but I can build great walls that can never be overthrown. Let me build the wall round your City."

"How long will it take you to build a wall that will go round our City?" said the Father of the Gods.

"A year, O Odin," said the Stranger.

Now Odin knew that if a great wall could be built around it the Gods would not have to spend all their time defending their City, Asgard, from the Giants, and he knew that if Asgard were protected, he himself could go amongst men and teach them and help them. He thought that no payment the Stranger could ask would be too much for the building of that wall.

That day the Stranger came to the Council of the Gods, and he swore that in a year he would have the great wall built. Then Odin made oath that the Gods would give him what he asked in payment if the wall was finished to the last stone in a year from that day.

The Stranger went away and came back on the morrow. It was the first day of Summer when he started work. He brought no one to help him except a great horse.

Now the Gods thought that this horse would do no more than drag blocks of stone for the building of the wall. But the horse did more than this. He set the stones in their places and mortared them together. And day and night and by light and dark the horse worked, and soon a great wall was rising round the palaces that the Gods themselves were building.

"What reward will the Stranger ask for the work he is doing for us?" the Gods asked one another.

Odin went to the Stranger. "We marvel at the work you and your horse are doing for us," he said. "No one can doubt that the great wall of Asgard will be built up by the first day of

Summer. What reward do you claim? We would have it ready for you."

The Stranger turned from the work he was doing, leaving the great horse to pile up the blocks of stone. "O Father of the Gods," he said, "O Odin, the reward I shall ask for my work is the Sun and the Moon, and Freya, who watches over the flowers and grasses, for my wife."

Now when Odin heard this he was terribly angered, for the price the Stranger asked for his work was beyond all prices. He went amongst the other Gods who were then building their shining palaces within the great wall and he told them what reward the Stranger had asked. The Gods said, "Without the Sun and the Moon the world will wither away." And the Goddesses said, "Without Freya all will be gloom in Asgard."

They would have let the wall remain unbuilt rather than let the Stranger have the reward he claimed for building it. But one who was in the company of the Gods spoke. He was Loki, a being who only half belonged to the Gods; his father was the Wind Giant. "Let the Stranger build the wall round Asgard," Loki said, "and I will find a way to make him give up the hard bargain he has made with the Gods. Go to him and tell him that the wall must be finished by the first day of Summer, and that if it is not finished to the last stone on that day the price he asks will not be given to him."

The Gods went to the Stranger and they told him that if the last stone was not laid on the wall on the first day of the Summer not Sol or Mani, the Sun and the Moon, nor Freya would be given him. And now they knew that the Stranger was one of the Giants.

The Giant and his great horse piled up the wall more quickly than before. At night, while the Giant slept, the horse worked on and on, hauling up stones and laying them on the wall with his great forefeet. And day by day the wall around Asgard grew higher and higher.

But the Gods had no joy in seeing that great wall rising higher and higher around their palaces. The Giant and his horse would finish the work by the first day of Summer, and then he would take the Sun and the Moon, Sol and Mani, and Freya away with him.

But Loki was not disturbed. He kept telling the Gods that he would find a way to prevent him from finishing his work, and thus he would make the Giant forfeit the terrible price he had led Odin to promise him.

It was three days to Summer time. All the wall was finished except the gateway. Over the gateway a stone was still to be placed. And the Giant, before he went to sleep, bade his horse haul up a great block of stone so that they might put it above the gateway in the morning, and so finish the work two full days before Summer.

It happened to be a beautiful moonlit night. Svadilfare, the Giant's great horse, was hauling the largest stone he ever hauled when he saw a little mare come galloping toward him. The great horse had never seen so pretty a little mare and he looked at her with surprise.

"Svadilfare, slave," said the little mare to him and went frisking past.

Svadilfare put down the stone he was hauling and called to the little mare. She came back to him. "Why do you call me 'Svadilfare, slave'?" said the great horse.

"Because you have to work night and day for your master," said the little mare. "He keeps you working, working, working, and never lets you enjoy yourself. You dare not leave that stone down and come and play with me."

"Who told you I dare not do it?" said Svadilfare.

"I know you daren't do it," said the little mare, and she kicked up her heels and ran across the moonlit meadow.

Now the truth is that Svadilfare was tired of working day and night. When he saw the little mare go galloping off he became suddenly discontented. He left the stone he was hauling on the ground. He looked round and he saw the little mare looking back at him. He galloped after her.

He did not catch up on the little mare. She went on swiftly before him. On she went over the moonlit meadow, turning and looking back now and again at the great Svadilfare, who came heavily after her. Down the mountainside the mare went, and Svadilfare, who now rejoiced in his liberty and in the freshness of the wind and in the smell of the flowers, still followed her. With the morning's light they came near a cave and the little mare went into it. They went through the cave. Then Svadilfare caught up on the little mare and the two went wandering together, the little mare telling Svadilfare stories of the Dwarfs and the Elves.

They came to a grove and they stayed together in it, the little mare playing so nicely with him that the great horse forgot all about time passing. And while they were in the grove the Giant was going up and down, searching for his great horse.

He had come to the wall in the morning, expecting to put the stone over the gateway and so finish his work. But the stone that was to be lifted up was not near him. He called for Svadilfare, but his great horse did not come. He went to search for him, and he searched all down the mountainside and he searched as far across the earth as the realm of the Giants. But he did not find Svadilfare.

The Gods saw the first day of Summer come and the gateway of the wall stand unfinished. They said to each other that if it were not finished by the evening they need not give

Sol and Mani to the Giant, nor the maiden Freya to be his wife. The hours of the summer day went past and the Giant did not raise the stone over the gateway. In the evening he came before them.

"Your work is not finished," Odin said. "You forced us to a hard bargain and now we need not keep it with you. You shall not be given Sol and Mani nor the maiden Freya."

"Only the wall I have built is so strong I would tear it down," said the Giant. He tried to throw down one of the palaces, but the Gods laid hands on him and thrust him outside the wall he had built. "Go, and trouble Asgard no more," Odin commanded.

Then Loki returned to Asgard. He told the Gods how he had transformed himself into a little mare and had led away Svadilfare, the Giant's great horse. And the Gods sat in their golden palaces behind the great wall and rejoiced that their City was now secure, and that no enemy could ever enter it or over-throw it. But Odin, the Father of the Gods, as he sat upon his throne was sad in his heart, sad that the Gods had got their wall built by a trick; that oaths had been broken, and that a blow had been struck in injustice in Asgard.

IDUNA AND HER APPLES: HOW LOKI PUT THE GODS IN DANGER

In Asgard there was a garden, and in that garden there grew a tree, and on that tree there grew shining apples. Thou know'st, O well-loved one, that every day that passes makes us older and brings us to that day when we will be bent and feeble, gray-headed and weak-eyed. But those shining apples that grew in Asgard—they who ate of them every day grew never a day older, for the eating of the apples kept old age away.

Iduna, the Goddess, tended the tree on which the shining apples grew. None would grow on the tree unless she was there to tend it. No one but Iduna might pluck the shining apples. Each morning she plucked them and left them in her basket and every day the Gods and Goddesses came to her garden that they might eat the shining apples and so stay forever Young.

Iduna never went from her garden. All day and every day she stayed in the garden or in her golden house beside it, and all day and every day she listened to Bragi, her husband, tell a story that never had an end.

Ah, but a time came when Iduna and her apples were lost

to Asgard, and the Gods and Goddesses felt old age approach them. How all that happened shall be told thee, O well beloved.

Odin, the Father of the Gods, often went into the land of men to watch over their doings. Once he took Loki with him, Loki, the doer of good and the doer of evil. For a long time they went traveling through the world of men. At last they came near Jötunheim, the realm of the Giants.

It was a bleak and empty region. There were no growing things there, not even trees with berries. There were no birds, there were no animals. As Odin, the Father of the Gods, and Loki, the doer of good and the doer of evil, went through this region hunger came upon them. But in all the land around they saw nothing that they could eat.

Loki, running here and running there, came at last upon a herd of wild cattle. Creeping up on them, he caught hold of a young bull and killed him. Then he cut up the flesh into strips of meat. He lighted a fire and put the meat on spits to roast. While the meat was being cooked, Odin, the Father of the Gods, a little way off, sat thinking on the things he had seen in the world of men.

Loki made himself busy putting more and more logs on the fire. At last he called to Odin, and the Father of the Gods came and sat down near the fire to eat the meal.

But when the meat was taken off the cooking-spits and when Odin went to cut it, he found that it was still raw. He smiled at Loki for thinking the meat was cooked, and Loki, troubled that he had made a mistake, put the meat back, and put more logs upon the fire. Again Loki took the meat off the cooking-spits and called Odin to the meal.

Odin, when he took the meat that Loki brought him, found that it was as raw as if it had never been put upon the fire. "Is this a trick of yours, Loki?" he said.

Loki was so angry at the meat being uncooked that Odin saw he was playing no tricks. In his hunger he raged at the meat and he raged at the fire. Again he put the meat on the cooking-spits and put more logs on the fire. Every hour he would take up the meat, sure that it was now cooked, and every time he took it off Odin would find that the meat was as raw as the first time they took it off the fire.

Now Odin knew that the meat must be under some enchantment by the Giants. He stood up and went on his way, hungry but strong. Loki, however, would not leave the meat that he had put back on the fire. He would make it be cooked, he declared, and he would not leave that place Hungry.

The dawn came and he took up the meat again. As he was lifting it off the fire he heard a whirr of wings above his head. Looking up, he saw a mighty eagle, the largest eagle that ever appeared in the sky. The eagle circled round and round and came above Loki's head.

"Canst thou not cook thy food?" the eagle screamed to him.

"I cannot cook it," said Loki.

"I will cook it for thee, if thou wilt give me a share," screamed the eagle.

"Come, then, and cook it for me," said Loki.

The eagle circled round until he was above the fire. Then flapping his great wings over it, he made the fire blaze and blaze. A heat that Loki had never felt before came from the burning logs. In a minute he drew the meat from the spits and found it was well cooked.

"My share, my share, give me my share," the eagle screamed at him. He flew down, and seizing on a large piece of meat instantly devoured it. He seized on another piece. Piece after piece he devoured until it looked as if Loki would be left with no meat for his meal.

As the eagle seized on the last piece Loki became angry

indeed. Taking up the spit on which the meat had been cooked, he struck at the eagle. There was a clang as if he had struck some metal. The wood of the spit did not come away. It stuck to the breast of the eagle. But Loki did not let go his hold on the spit. Suddenly the eagle rose up in the air. Loki, who held to the spit that was fastened to the eagle's breast, was drawn up with him.

Before he knew what had happened Loki was miles and miles up in the air and the eagle was flying with him toward Jötunheim, the Realm of the Giants. And the eagle was screaming out, "Loki, friend Loki, I have thee at last. It was thou who didst cheat my brother of his reward for building the wall round Asgard. But, Loki, I have thee at last. Know now that Thiassi the Giant has captured thee, O Loki, most cunning of the dwellers in Asgard."

Thus the eagle screamed as he went flying with Loki toward Jötunheim, the Realm of the Giants. They passed over the river that divides Jötunheim from Midgard, the World of Men. And now Loki saw a terrible place beneath him, a land of ice and rock. Great mountains were there: they were lighted by neither sun nor moon, but by columns of fire thrown up now and again through cracks in the earth or out of the peaks of the mountains.

Over a great iceberg the eagle hovered. Suddenly he shook the spit from his breast and Loki fell down on the ice. The eagle screamed out to him, "Thou art in my power at last, O thou most cunning of all the Dwellers in Asgard." The eagle left Loki there and flew within a crack in the mountain.

Miserable indeed was Loki upon that iceberg. The cold was deadly. He could not die there, for he was one of the Dwellers in Asgard and death might not come to him that way. He might not die, but he felt bound to that iceberg with chains of cold.

After a day his captor came to him, not as an eagle this time, but in his own form, Thiassi the Giant.

"Wouldst thou leave thine iceberg, Loki," he said, "and return to thy pleasant place in Asgard? Thou dost delight in Asgard, although only by one-half dost thou belong to the Gods. Thy father, Loki, was the Wind Giant."

"O that I might leave this iceberg," Loki said, with the tears freezing on his face.

"Thou mayst leave it when thou showest thyself ready to pay thy ransom to me," said Thiassi. "Thou wilt have to get me the shining apples that Iduna keeps in her basket."

"I cannot get Iduna's apples for thee, Thiassi," said Loki.

"Then stay upon the iceberg," said Thiassi the Giant. He went away and left Loki there with the terrible winds buffeting him as with blows of a hammer.

When Thiassi came again and spoke to him about his ransom, Loki said, "There is no way of getting the shining apples from Iduna."

"There must be some way, O cunning Loki," said the Giant.

"Iduna, although she guards well the shining apples, is simple-minded," said Loki. "It may be that I shall be able to get her to go outside the wall of Asgard. If she goes she will bring her shining apples with her, for she never lets them go out of her hand except when she gives them to the Gods and Goddesses to eat."

"Make it so that she will go beyond the wall of Asgard," said the Giant. "If she goes outside of the wall I shall get the apples from her. Swear by the World-Tree that thou wilt lure Iduna beyond the wall of Asgard. Swear it, Loki, and I shall let thee go."

"I swear it by Ygdrassil, the World-Tree, that I will lure Iduna beyond the wall of Asgard if thou wilt take me off this iceberg," said Loki.

Then Thiassi changed himself into a mighty eagle, and taking Loki in his talons, he flew with him over the stream that divides Jötunheim, the Realm of the Giants, from Midgard, the World of Men. He left Loki on the ground of Midgard, and Loki then went on his way to Asgard.

Now Odin had already returned and he had told the Dwellers in Asgard of Loki's attempt to cook the enchanted meat. All laughed to think that Loki had been left hungry for all his cunning. Then when he came into Asgard looking so famished, they thought it was because Loki had had nothing to eat. They laughed at him more and more. But they brought him into the Feast Hall and they gave him the best of food with wine out of Odin's wine cup. When the feast was over the Dwellers in Asgard went to Iduna's garden as was their wont.

There sat Iduna in the golden house that opened on her garden. Had she been in the world of men, everyone who saw her would have remembered their own innocence, seeing one who was so fair and good. She had eyes blue as the blue sky, and she smiled as if she were remembering lovely things she had seen or heard. The basket of shining apples was beside her.

To each God and Goddess Iduna gave a shining apple. Each one ate the apple given, rejoicing to think that they would never become a day older. Then Odin, the Father of the Gods, said the runes that were always said in praise of Iduna, and the Dwellers in Asgard went out of Iduna's garden, each one going to his or her own shining house.

All went except Loki, the doer of good and the doer of evil. Loki sat in the garden, watching fair and simple Iduna. After a while she spoke to him and said, "Why dost thou still stay here, wise Loki?"

"To look well on thine apples," Loki said. "I am wondering if the apples I saw yesterday are really as shining as the apples that are in thy basket."

"There are no apples in the world as shining as mine," said Iduna.

"The apples I saw were more shining," said Loki. "Aye, and they smelled better, Iduna."

Iduna was troubled at what Loki, whom she deemed so wise, told her. Her eyes filled with tears that there might be more shining apples in the world than hers. "O Loki," she said, "it cannot be. No apples are more shining, and none smell so sweet, as the apples I pluck off the tree in my garden."

"Go, then, and see," said Loki. "Just outside Asgard is the tree that has the apples I saw. Thou, Iduna, dost never leave thy garden, and so thou dost not know what grows in the world. Go outside of Asgard and see."

"I will go, Loki," said Iduna, the fair and simple.

Iduna went outside the wall of Asgard. She went to the place Loki had told her that the apples grew in. But as she looked this way and that way, Iduna heard a whirr of wings above her. Looking up, she saw a mighty eagle, the largest eagle that had ever appeared in the sky.

She drew back toward the gate of Asgard. Then the great eagle swooped down; Iduna felt herself lifted up, and then she was being carried away from Asgard, away, away; away over Midgard where men lived, away toward the rocks and snows of Jötunheim. Across the river that flows between the World of Men and the Realm of the Giants Iduna was borne. Then the eagle flew into a cleft in a mountain and Iduna was left in a cavernous hall lighted up by columns of fire that burst up from the earth.

The eagle loosened his grip on Iduna and she sank down on the ground of the cavern. The wings and the feathers fell from him and she saw her captor as a terrible Giant.

"Oh, why have you carried me off from Asgard and brought me to this place?" Iduna cried.

"That I might eat your shining apples, Iduna," said Thiassi the Giant.

"That will never be, for I will not give them to you," said Iduna.

"Give me the apples to eat, and I shall carry you back to Asgard."

"No, no, that cannot be. I have been trusted with the shining apples that I might give them to the Gods only."

"Then I shall take the apples from you," said Thiassi the Giant.

He took the basket out of her hands and opened it. But when he touched the apples they shriveled under his hands. He left them in the basket and he set the basket down, for he knew now that the apples would be no good to him unless Iduna gave them to him with her own hands.

"You must stay with me here until you give me the shining apples," he said to her.

Then was poor Iduna frightened: she was frightened of the strange cave and frightened of the fire that kept bursting up out of the earth and she was frightened of the terrible Giant. But above all she was frightened to think of the evil that would fall upon the Dwellers in Asgard if she were not there to give them the shining apples to eat.

The Giant came to her again. But still Iduna would not give him the shining apples. And there in the cave she stayed, the Giant troubling her every day. And she grew more and more fearful as she saw in her dreams the Dwellers in Asgard go to her garden—go there, and not being given the shining apples, feel and see a change coming over themselves and over each other.

It was as Iduna saw it in her dreams. Every day the Dwellers in Asgard went to her garden—Odin and Thor, Hödur and Baldur, Tyr and Heimdall, Vidar and Vali, with Frigga,

Freya, Nanna, and Sif. There was no one to pluck the apples of their tree. And a change began to come over the Gods and Goddesses.

They no longer walked lightly; their shoulders became bent; their eyes no longer were as bright as dewdrops. And when they looked upon one another they saw the change. Age was coming upon the Dwellers in Asgard.

They knew that the time would come when Frigga would be gray and old; when Sif's golden hair would fade; when Odin would no longer have his clear wisdom, and when Thor would not have strength enough to raise and fling his thunderbolts. And the Dwellers in Asgard were saddened by this knowledge, and it seemed to them that all brightness had gone from their shining City.

Where was Iduna whose apples would give back youth and strength and beauty to the Dwellers in Asgard? The Gods had searched for her through the World of Men. No trace of her did they find. But now Odin, searching through his wisdom, saw a means to get knowledge of where Iduna was hidden.

He summoned his two ravens, Hugin and Munin, his two ravens that flew through the earth and through the Realm of the Giants and that knew all things that were past and all things that were to come. He summoned Hugin and Munin and they came, and one sat on his right shoulder and one sat on his left shoulder and they told him deep secrets: they told him of Thiassi and of his desire for the shining apples that the Dwellers in Asgard ate, and of Loki's deception of Iduna, the fair and simple.

What Odin learnt from his ravens was told in the Council of the Gods. Then Thor the Strong went to Loki and laid hands upon him. When Loki found himself in the grip of the strong God, he said, "What wouldst thou with me, O Thor?"

"I would hurl thee into a chasm in the ground and strike

thee with my thunder," said the strong God. "It was thou who didst bring it about that Iduna went from Asgard."

"O Thor," said Loki, "do not crush me with thy thunder. Let me stay in Asgard. I will strive to win Iduna back."

"The judgment of the Gods," said Thor, "is that thou, the cunning one, shouldst go to Jötunheim, and by thy craft win Iduna back from the Giants. Go or else I shall hurl thee into a chasm and crush thee with my thunder."

"I will go," said Loki.

From Frigga, the wife of Odin, Loki borrowed the dress of falcon feathers that she owned. He clad himself in it, and flew to Jötunheim in the form of a falcon.

He searched through Jötunheim until he found Thiassi's daughter, Skadi. He flew before Skadi and he let the Giant maid catch him and hold him as a pet. One day the Giant maid carried him into the cave where Iduna, the fair and simple, was held.

When Loki saw Iduna there he knew that part of his quest was ended. Now he had to get Iduna out of Jötunheim and away to Asgard. He stayed no more with the Giant maid, but flew up into the high rocks of the cave. Skadi wept for the flight of her pet, but she ceased to search and to call and went away from the cave.

Then Loki, the doer of good and the doer of evil, flew to where Iduna was sitting and spoke to her. Iduna, when she knew that one of the Dwellers in Asgard was near, wept with joy.

Loki told her what she was to do. By the power of a spell that was given him he was able to change her into the form of a sparrow. But before she did this she took the shining apples out of her basket and flung them into places where the Giant would never find them.

Skadi, coming back to the cave, saw the falcon fly out with

the sparrow beside him. She cried out to her father and the Giant knew that the falcon was Loki and the sparrow was Iduna. He changed himself into the form of a mighty eagle. By this time sparrow and falcon were out of sight, but Thiassi, knowing that he could make better flight than they, flew toward Asgard.

Soon he saw them. They flew with all the power they had, but the great wings of the eagle brought him nearer and nearer to them. The Dwellers in Asgard, standing on the wall, saw the falcon and the sparrow with the great eagle pursuing them. They knew who they were—Loki and Iduna with Thiassi in pursuit.

As they watched the eagle winging nearer and nearer, the Dwellers in Asgard were fearful that the falcon and the sparrow would be caught upon and that Iduna would be taken again by Thiassi. They lighted great fires upon the wall, knowing that Loki would find a way through the fires, bringing Iduna with him, but that Thiassi would not find a way.

The falcon and the sparrow flew toward the fires. Loki went between the flames and brought Iduna with him. And Thiassi, coming up to the fires and finding no way through, beat his wings against the flames. He fell down from the wall and the death that came to him afterwards was laid to Loki.

Thus Iduna was brought back to Asgard. Once again she sat in the golden house that opened to her garden, once again she plucked the shining apples off the tree she tended, and once again she gave them to the Dwellers in Asgard. And the Dwellers in Asgard walked lightly again, and brightness came into their eyes and into their cheeks; age no more approached them; youth came back; light and joy were again in Asgard.

SIF'S GOLDEN HAIR: HOW LOKI WROUGHT MISCHIEF IN ASGARD

All who dwelt in Asgard, the Æsir and the Asyniur, who were the Gods and the Goddesses, and the Vanir, who were the friends of the Gods and the Goddesses, were wroth with Loki. It was no wonder they were wroth with him, for he had let the Giant Thiassi carry off Iduna and her golden apples. Still, it must be told that the show they made of their wrath made Loki ready to do more mischief in Asgard.

One day he saw a chance to do mischief that made his heart rejoice. Sif, the wife of Thor, was lying asleep outside her house. Her beautiful golden hair flowed all round her. Loki knew how much Thor loved that shining hair, and how greatly Sif prized it because of Thor's love. Here was his chance to do a great mischief. Smilingly, he took out his shears and he cut off the shining hair, every strand and every tress. She did not waken while her treasure was being taken from her. But Loki left Sif's head cropped and bare.

Thor was away from Asgard. Coming back to the City of the Gods, he went into his house. Sif, his wife, was not there to welcome him. He called to Sif, but no glad answer came from her. To the palaces of all the Gods and Goddesses Thor went, but in none of them did he find Sif, his golden-haired wife.

When he was coming back to his house he heard his name whispered. He stopped, and then a figure stole out from behind a stone. A veil covered her head, and Thor scarce knew that this was Sif, his wife. As he went to her she sobbed and sobbed. "O Thor, my husband," she said, "do not look upon me. I am ashamed that you should see me. I shall go from Asgard and from the company of the Gods and Goddesses, and I shall go down to Svartheim and live amongst the Dwarfs. I cannot bear that any of the Dwellers in Asgard should look upon me now."

"O Sif," cried Thor, "what has happened to change you?"

"I have lost the hair of my head," said Sif, "I have lost the beautiful golden hair that you, Thor, loved. You will not love me any more, and so I must go away, down to Svartheim and to the company of the Dwarfs. They are as ugly as I am now."

Then she took the veil off her head and Thor saw that all her beautiful hair was gone. She stood before him, shamed and sorrowful, and he grew into a mighty rage. "Who was it did this to you, Sif?" he said. "I am Thor, the strongest of all the Dwellers in Asgard, and I shall see to it that all the powers the Gods possess will be used to get your fairness back. Come with me, Sif." And taking his wife's hand in his, Thor went off to the Council House where the Gods and the Goddesses were.

Sif covered her head with her veil, for she would not have the Gods and Goddesses look upon her shorn head. But from the anger in Thor's eyes all saw that the wrong done to Sif was great indeed. Then Thor told of the cutting of her beautiful hair. A whisper went round the Council House. "It was Loki did this—no one else in Asgard would have done a deed so shameful," one said to the other.

"Loki it was who did it," said Thor. "He has hidden himself, but I shall find him and I will slay him."

"Nay, not so, Thor," said Odin, the Father of the Gods. "Nay, no Dweller in Asgard may slay another. I shall summon Loki to come before us here. It is for you to make him (and remember that Loki is cunning and able to do many things) bring back to Sif the beauty of her golden hair."

Then the call of Odin, the call that all in Asgard have to harken to, went through the City of the Gods. Loki heard it, and he had to come from his hiding-place and enter the house where the Gods held their Council. And when he looked on Thor and saw the rage that was in his eyes, and when he looked on Odin and saw the sternness in the face of the Father of the Gods, he knew that he would have to make amends for the shameful wrong he had done to Sif.

Said Odin, "There is a thing that you, Loki, have to do: Restore to Sif the beauty of her hair."

Loki looked at Odin, Loki looked at Thor, and he saw that what was said would have to be done. His quick mind searched to find a way of restoring to Sif the beauty of her golden hair.

"I shall do as you command, Odin All-Father," he said.

But before we tell you of what Loki did to restore the beauty of Sif's golden hair, we must tell you of the other beings besides the Gods and the Goddesses who were in the world at the time. First, there was the Vanir. When the Gods who were called the Æsir came to the mountain on which they built Asgard, they found other beings there. These were not wicked and ugly like the Giants; they were beautiful and friendly; the Vanir they were named.

Although they were beautiful and friendly the Vanir had no thought of making the world more beautiful or more happy. In that way they differed from the Æsir who had such a thought. The Æsir made peace with them, and they lived together in friendship, and the Vanir came to do things that helped the Æsir to make the world more beautiful and more happy. Freya, whom the Giant wanted to take away with the Sun and the Moon as a reward for the building of the wall round Asgard, was of the Vanir. The other beings of the Vanir were Frey, who was the brother of Freya, and Niörd, who was their father.

On the earth below there were other beings—the dainty Elves, who danced and fluttered about, attending to the trees and flowers and grasses. The Vanir were permitted to rule over the Elves. Then below the earth, in caves and hollows, there was another race, the Dwarfs or Gnomes, little, twisted creatures, who were both wicked and ugly, but who were the best craftsmen in the world.

In the days when neither the Æsir nor the Vanir were friendly to him Loki used to go down to Svartheim, the Dwarfs' dwelling below the earth. And now that he was commanded to restore to Sif the beauty of her hair, Loki thought of help he might get from the Dwarfs.

Down, down, through the winding passages in the earth he went, and he came at last to where the Dwarfs who were most friendly to him were working in their forges. All the Dwarfs were master-smiths, and when he came upon his friends he found them working hammer and tongs, beating metals into many shapes. He watched them for a while and took note of the things they were making. One was a spear, so well balanced and made that it would hit whatever mark it was thrown at no matter how bad the aim the thrower had. The other was a boat that could sail on any sea, but that could be folded up so that it would go into one's pocket. The spear was called Gungnir and the boat was called Skidbladnir.

Loki made himself very agreeable to the Dwarfs, praising their work and promising them things that only the Dwellers in Asgard could give, things that the Dwarfs longed to possess.

He talked to them till the little, ugly folk thought that they would come to own Asgard and all that was in it.

At last Loki said to them, "Have you got a bar of fine gold that you can hammer into threads—into threads so fine that they will be like the hair of Sif, Thor's wife? Only the Dwarfs could make a thing so wonderful. Ah, there is the bar of gold. Hammer it into those fine threads, and the Gods themselves will be jealous of your work."

Flattered by Loki's speeches, the Dwarfs who were in the forge took up the bar of fine gold and flung it into the fire. Then taking it out and putting it upon their anvil they worked on the bar with their tiny hammers until they beat it into threads that were as fine as the hairs of one's head. But that was not enough. They had to be as fine as the hairs on Sif's head, and these were finer than anything else. They worked on the threads, over and over again, until they were as fine as the hairs on Sif's head. The threads were as bright as sunlight, and when Loki took up the mass of worked gold it flowed from his raised hand down on the ground. It was so fine that it could be put into his palm, and it was so light that a bird might not feel its weight.

Then Loki praised the Dwarfs more and more, and he made more and more promises to them. He charmed them all, although they were an unfriendly and a suspicious folk. And before he left them he asked them for the spear and the boat he had seen them make, the spear Gungnir and the boat Skidbladnir. The Dwarfs gave him these things, though in a while after they wondered at themselves for giving them.

Back to Asgard Loki went. He walked into the Council House where the Dwellers in Asgard were gathered. He met the stern look in Odin's eyes and the rageful look in Thor's eyes with smiling good humor. "Off with thy veil, O Sif," he said. And when poor Sif took off her veil he put upon her shorn head the wonderful mass of gold he held in his palm. Over her shoulders the gold fell, fine, soft, and shining as her own hair. And the Æsir and the Asyniur, the Gods and the Goddesses, and the Van and Vana, when they saw Sif's head covered again with the shining web, laughed and clapped their hands in gladness. And the shining web held to Sif's head as if indeed it had roots and was growing there.

How Brock Brought Judgement on Loki

It was then that Loki, with the wish of making the Æsir and the Vanir friendly to him once more, brought out the wonderful things he had gained from the Dwarfs—the spear Gungnir and the boat Skidbladnir. The Æsir and the Vanir marveled at things so wonderful. Loki gave the spear as a gift to Odin, and to Frey, who was chief of the Vanir, he gave the boat Skidbladnir.

All Asgard rejoiced that things so wonderful and so helpful had been brought to them. And Loki, who had made a great show in giving these gifts, said boastingly:

"None but the Dwarfs who work for me could make such things. There are other Dwarfs, but they are as unhandy as they are misshapen. The Dwarfs who are my servants are the only ones who can make such wonders."

Now Loki in his boastfulness had said a foolish thing. There were other Dwarfs besides those who had worked for him, and one of these was there in Asgard. All unknown to Loki he stood in the shadow of Odin's seat, listening to what was being said. Now he went over to Loki, his little, unshapely form

"

trembling with rage—Brock, the most spiteful of all the Dwarfs.

"Ha, Loki, you boaster," he roared, "you lie in your words. Sindri, my brother, who would scorn to serve you, is the best smith in Svartheim."

The Æsir and the Vanir laughed to see Loki outfaced by Brock the Dwarf in the middle of his boastfulness. As they laughed Loki grew angry.

"Be silent, Dwarf," he said, "your brother will know about smith's work when he goes to the Dwarfs who are my friends, and learns something from them."

"He learns from the Dwarfs who are your friends! My brother Sindri learn from the Dwarfs who are your friends!" Brock roared, in a greater rage than before. "The things you have brought out of Svartheim would not be noticed by the Æsir and the Vanir if they were put beside the things that my brother Sindri can make."

"Sometime we will try your brother Sindri and see what he can do," said Loki.

"Try now, try now," Brock shouted. "I'll wager my head against yours, Loki, that his work will make the Dwellers in Asgard laugh at your boasting."

"I will take your wager," said Loki. "My head against yours. And glad will I be to see that ugly head of yours off your misshapen shoulders."

"The Æsir will judge whether my brother's work is not the best that ever came out of Svartheim. And they will see to it that you will pay your wager, Loki, the head off your shoulders. Will ye not sit in judgment, O Dwellers in Asgard?"

"We will sit in judgment," said the Æsir. Then, still full of rage, Brock the Dwarf went down to Svartheim, and to the place where his brother Sindri worked.

There was Sindri in his glowing forge, working with

bellows and anvil and hammers beside him, and around him masses of metal—gold and silver, copper and iron. Brock told his tale, how he had wagered his head against Loki's that Sindri could make things more wonderful than the spear and the boat that Loki had brought into Asgard.

"You were right in what you said, my brother," said Sindri, "and you shall not lose your head to Loki. But the two of us must work at what I am going to forge. It will be your work to keep the fire so that it will neither blaze up nor die down for a single instant. If you can keep the fire as I tell you, we will forge a wonder. Now, brother, keep your hands upon the bellows, and keep the fire under your control."

Then into the fire Sindri threw, not a piece of metal, but a pig's skin. Brock kept his hands on the bellows, working it so that the fire neither died down nor blazed up for a single instant. And in the glowing fire the pigskin swelled itself into a strange shape.

But Brock was not left to work the bellows in peace. Into the forge flew a gad-fly. It lighted on Brock's hands and stung them. The Dwarf screamed with pain, but his hands still held the bellows, working it to keep the fire steady, for he knew that the gad-fly was Loki, and that Loki was striving to spoil Sindri's work. Again the gad-fly stung his hands, but Brock, although his hands felt as if they were pierced with hot irons, still worked the bellows so that the fire did not blaze up or die down for a single instant.

Sindri came and looked into the fire. Over the shape that was rising there he said words of magic. The gad-fly had flown away, and Sindri bade his brother cease working. He took out the thing that had been shaped in the fire, and he worked over it with his hammer. It was a wonder indeed—a boar, all golden, that could fly through the air, and that shed light from its bristles as it flew. Brock forgot the pain in his hands and screamed with joy. "This is the greatest of wonders," he said. "The Dwellers in Asgard will have to give the judgment against Loki. I shall have Loki's head! I shall have Loki's head!"

But Sindri said, "The boar Golden Bristle may not be judged as great a wonder as the spear Gungnir or the boat Skidbladnir. We must make something more wonderful still. Work the bellows as before, brother, and do not let the fire die down or blaze up for a single instant."

Then Sindri took up a piece of gold that was so bright it lightened up the dark cavern that the Dwarfs worked in. He threw the piece of gold into the fire. Then he went to make ready something else and left Brock to work the bellows.

The gad-fly flew in again. Brock did not know it was there until it lighted on the back of his neck. It stung him till Brock felt the pain was wrenching him apart. But still he kept his hands on the bellows, working it so that the fire neither blazed up nor died down for a single instant. When Sindri came to look into the fire, Brock was not able to speak for pain.

Again Sindri said magic words over the gold that was being smelted in the fire. He took it out of the glow and worked it over on the main-anvil. Then in a while he showed Brock something that looked like the circle of their sun. "A splendid arm-ring, my brother," he said. "An arm-ring for a God's right arm. And this ring has hidden wonders. Every ninth night eight rings like itself will drop from this arm-ring, for this is Draupnir, the Ring of Increase."

"To Odin, the Father of the Gods, the ring shall be given," said Brock. "And Odin will have to declare that nothing so wonderful or so profitable to the Gods was ever brought into Asgard. O Loki, cunning Loki, I shall have thy head in spite of thy tricks."

"Be not too hasty, brother," said Sindri. "What we have done so far is good. But better still must be the thing that will make the Dwellers in Asgard give the judgment that delivers Loki's head to thee. Work as before, brother, and do not let the fire blaze up or die down for a single instant."

This time Sindri threw into the fire a bar of iron. Then he went away to fetch the hammer that would shape it. Brock worked the bellows as before, but only his hands were steady, for every other part of him was trembling with expectation of the gad-fly's sting.

He saw the gad-fly dart into the forge. He screamed as it flew round and round him, searching out a place where it might sting him most fearfully. It lighted down on his forehead, just between his eyes. The first sting it gave took the sight from his eyes. It stung again and Brock felt the blood flowing down. Darkness filled the cave. Brock tried to keep his hands steady on the bellows, but he did not know whether the fire was blazing up or dying down. He shouted and Sindri hurried up.

Sindri said the magic words over the thing that was in the fire. Then he drew it out. "An instant more," he said, "and the work would have been perfect. But because you let the fire die down for an instant the work is not as good as it might have been made." He took what was shaped in the fire to the main-anvil and worked over it. Then when Brock's eyesight came back to him he saw a great hammer, a hammer all of iron. The handle did not seem to be long enough to balance the head. This was because the fire had died down for an instant while it was being formed.

"The hammer is Miölnir," said Sindri, "and it is the greatest of the things that I am able to make. All in Asgard must rejoice to see this hammer. Thor only will be able to wield it. Now I am not afraid of the judgment that the Dwellers in Asgard will give."

"The Dwellers in Asgard will have to give judgment for us,"

Brock cried out. "They will have to give judgment for us, and the head of Loki, my tormentor, will be given me."

"No more wonderful or more profitable gifts than these have ever been brought into Asgard," Sindri said. "Thy head is saved, and thou wilt be able to take the head of Loki who was insolent to us. Bring it here, and we will throw it into the fire in the forge."

The Æsir and the Vanir were seated in the Council House of Asgard when a train of Dwarfs appeared before them. Brock came at the head of the train, and he was followed by a band of Dwarfs carrying things of great weight. Brock and his attendants stood round the throne of Odin, and hearkened to the words of the Father of the Gods.

"We know why you have come into Asgard from out of Svartheim," Odin said. "You have brought things wonderful and profitable to the Dwellers in Asgard. Let what you have brought be seen, Brock. If they are more wonderful and more useful than the things Loki has brought out of Svartheim, the spear Gungnir and the boat Skidbladnir, we will give judgment for you."

Then Brock commanded the Dwarfs who waited on him to show the Dwellers in Asgard the first of the wonders that Sindri had made. They brought out the boar, Golden Bristle. Round and round the Council House the boar flew, leaving a track of brightness. The Dwellers in Asgard said one to the other that this was a wonder indeed. But none would say that the boar was a better thing to have in Asgard than the spear that would hit the mark no matter how badly it was flung, or the boat Skidbladnir that would sail on any sea, and that could be folded up so small that it would fit in any one's pocket: none would say that Golden Bristle was better than these wonders.

To Frey, who was Chief of the Vanir, Brock gave the wondrous boar.

Then the attending Dwarfs showed the arm-ring that was as bright as the circle of the Sun. All admired the noble ring. And when it was told how every ninth night this ring dropped eight rings of gold that were like itself, the Dwellers in Asgard spoke aloud, all saying that Draupnir, the Ring of Increase, was a wonder indeed. Hearing their voices raised, Brock looked triumphantly at Loki who was standing there with his lips drawn closely together.

To Odin, the Father of the Gods, Brock gave the noble arm-ring.

Then he commanded the attending Dwarfs to lay before Thor the hammer Miölnir. Thor took the hammer up and swung it around his head. As he did so he uttered a great cry. And the eyes of the Dwellers in Asgard lightened up when they saw Thor with the hammer Miölnir in his hands; their eyes lightened up and from their lips came the cry, "This is a wonder, a wonder indeed! With this hammer in his hand none can withstand Thor, our Champion. No greater thing has ever come into Asgard than the hammer Miölnir."

Then Odin, the Father of the Gods, spoke from his throne, giving judgment. "The hammer Miölnir that the Dwarf Brock has brought into Asgard is a thing wonderful indeed and profitable to the Gods. In Thor's hands it can crush mountains, and hurl the Giant race from the ramparts of Asgard. Sindri the Dwarf has forged a greater thing than the spear Gungnir and the boat Skidbladnir. There can be no other judgment."

Brock looked at Loki, showing his gnarled teeth. "Now, Loki, yield your head, yield your head," he cried.

"Do not ask such a thing," said Odin. "Put any other penalty on Loki for mocking you and tormenting you. Make him yield to you the greatest thing that it is in his power to give."

"Not so, not so," screamed Brock. "You Dwellers in Asgard

would shield one another. But what of me? Loki would have taken my head had I lost the wager. Loki has lost his head to me. Let him kneel down now till I cut it off."

Loki came forward, smiling with closed lips. "I kneel before you, Dwarf," he said. "Take off my head. But be careful. Do not touch my neck. I did not bargain that you should touch my neck. If you do, I shall call upon the Dwellers in Asgard to punish you."

Brock drew back with a snarl. "Is this the judgment of the Gods?" he asked.

"The bargain you made, Brock," said Odin, "was an evil one, and all its evil consequences you must bear."

Brock, in a rage, looked upon Loki, and he saw that his lips were smiling. He stamped his feet and raged. Then he went up to Loki and said, "I may not take your head, but I can do something with your lips that mock me."

"What would you do, Dwarf?" asked Thor.

"Sew Loki's lips together," said Brock, "so that he can do no more mischief with his talk. You Dwellers in Asgard cannot forbid me to do this. Down, Loki, on your knees before me."

Loki looked round on the Dwellers in Asgard and he saw that their judgment was that he must kneel before the Dwarf. He knelt down with a frown upon his brow. "Draw your lips together, Loki," said Brock. Loki drew his lips together while his eyes flashed fire. With an awl that he took from his belt Brock pierced Loki's lips. He took out a thong and tightened them together. Then in triumph the Dwarf looked on Loki.

"O Loki," he said, "you boasted that the Dwarfs who worked for you were better craftsmen than Sindri, my brother. Your words have been shown to be lies. And now you cannot boast for a while."

Then Brock the Dwarf, with great majesty, walked out of the Council House of Asgard, and the attending Dwarfs marched behind him in procession. Down the passages in the earth the Dwarfs went, singing the song of Brock's triumph over Loki. And in Svartheim it was told forever after how Sindri and Brock had prevailed.

In Asgard, now that Loki's lips were closed, there was peace and a respite from mischief. No one amongst the Æsir or the Vanir were sorry when Loki had to walk about in silence with his head bent low.

PART TWO
THOR AND LOKI AND THE GIANTS

THOR AND LOKI IN THE GIANTS' CITY

All but a few of the Dwellers of Asgard had come to the feast offered by Ægir the Old, the Giant King of the Sea. Frigga, the queenly wife of Odin, was there, and Frey and Freya; Iduna, who guarded the Apples of Youth, and Bragi, her husband; Tyr, the great swordsman, and Niörd, the God of the Sea, Skadi, who wedded Niörd and whose hatred for Loki was fierce, and Sif, whose golden hair was once shorn off by Loki the mischievous. Thor and Loki were there. The Dwellers of Asgard, gathered together in the hall of Ægir, waited for Odin.

Before Odin came Loki made the company merry by the tales that he told in mockery of Thor. Loki long since had his lips unloosed from the thong that the Dwarf Brock had sewn them with. And Thor had forgotten the wrong that he had done to Sif. Loki had been with Thor in his wanderings through Jötunheim, and about these wanderings he now told mocking tales.

He told how he had seen Thor in his chariot of brass drawn by two goats go across Bifröst, the Rainbow Bridge. None of the

Æsir or the Vanir knew on what adventure Thor was bent. But Loki followed him and Thor kept him in his company.

As they traveled on in the brass chariot drawn by the two goats, Thor told Loki of the adventure on which he was bent. He would go into Jötunheim, even into Utgard, the Giants' City, and he would try his strength against the Giants. He was not afraid of aught that might happen, for he carried Miölnir, his hammer, with him.

Their way was through Midgard, the World of Men. Once, as they were traveling on, night came upon them as they were hungry and in need of shelter. They saw a peasant's hut and they drove the chariot toward it. Unyoking the goats and leaving them standing in a hollow beside the chariot, the two, looking not like Dwellers in Asgard, but like men traveling through the country, knocked at the door of the hut and asked for food and shelter.

They could have shelter, the peasant and his wife told them, but they could not have food. There was little in that place, and what little there had been they had eaten for supper. The peasant showed them the inside of the hut: it was poor and bare, and there was nothing there to give anyone. In the morning, the peasant said, he would go down to the river and catch some fish for a meal.

"We can't wait until morning, we must eat now," said Thor, "and I think I can provide a good meal for us all." He went over to where his goats stood in the hollow beside the chariot of brass, and, striking them with his hammer, he left them lifeless on the ground. He skinned the goats then, and taking up the bones very carefully, he left them down on the skins. Skins and bones he lifted up and bringing them into the house he left them in a hole above the peasant's fireplace. "No one," said he in a commanding voice, "must touch the bones that I leave here."

Then he brought the meat into the house. Soon it was cooked and laid smoking on the table. The peasant and his wife and his son sat round the board with Thor and Loki. They had not eaten plentifully for many days, and now the man and the woman fed themselves well.

Thialfi was the name of the peasant's son. He was a growing lad and had an appetite that had not been satisfied for long. While the meat was on the table his father and mother had kept him going here and there, carrying water, putting fagots on the fire, and holding a blazing stick so that those at the table might see to eat. There was not much left for him when he was able to sit down, for Thor and Loki had great appetites, and the lad's father and mother had eaten to make up for days of want. So Thialfi got little out of that plentiful feast.

When the meal was finished they lay down on the benches. Thor, because he had made a long journey that day, slept very soundly. Thialfi lay down on a bench, too, but his thoughts were still upon the food. When all were asleep, he thought, he would take one of the bones that were in the skins above him, and break and gnaw it.

So in the dead of the night the lad stood up on the bench and took down the goat-skins that Thor had left so carefully there. He took out a bone, broke it, and gnawed it for the marrow. Loki was awake and saw him do this, but he, relishing mischief as much as ever, did nothing to stay the lad.

He put the bone he had broken back in the skins and he left the skins back in the hole above the fireplace. Then he went to sleep on the bench.

In the morning, as soon as they were up, the first thing Thor did was to take the skins out of the hole. He carried them carefully out to the hollow where he had left the goats stand- ing. He put each goat-skin down with the bones in it. He struck each with his hammer, and the goats sprang up alive, horns and hoofs and all.

But one was not as he had been before. He limped badly. Thor examined the leg and found out that one bone was broken. In terrible anger he turned on the peasant, his wife, and his son. "A bone of this goat has been broken under your roof," he shouted. "For that I shall destroy your house and leave you all dead under it."

Thialfi wept. Then he came forward and touched the knees of Thor. "I did not know what harm I did," he said. "I broke the bone."

Thor had his hammer lifted up to crush him into the earth. But he could not bring it down on the weeping boy. He let his hammer rest on the ground again. "You will have to do much service for me for having lamed my goat," he said. "Come with me."

And so the lad Thialfi went off with Thor and Loki. Thor took in his powerful hands the shafts of the chariot of brass and he dragged it into a lonely mountain hollow where neither men nor Giants came. And they left the goats in a great, empty forest to stay resting there until Thor called to them again.

Thor and Loki and the lad Thialfi went across from Midgard into Jötunheim. Because of Miölnir, the great hammer that he carried, Thor felt safe in the Realm of the Giants. And Loki, who trusted in his own cunning, felt safe, too. The lad Thialfi trusted in Thor so much that he had no fear. They were long in making the journey, and while they were traveling Thor and Loki trained Thialfi to be a quick and a strong lad.

One day they came out on a moor. All day they crossed it, and at night it still stretched far before them. A great wind was blowing, night was falling, and they saw no shelter near. In the dusk they saw a shape that looked to be a mountain and they went toward it, hoping to find some shelter in a cave.

Then Loki saw a lower shape that looked as if it might be a shelter. They walked around it, Loki and Thor and the lad Thialfi. It was a house, but a house most oddly shaped. The entrance was a long, wide hall that had no doorway. When they entered this hall they found five long and narrow chambers running off it. "It is an odd place, but it is the best shelter we can get," Loki said. "You and I, Thor, will take the two longest rooms, and the lad Thialfi can take one of the little rooms."

They entered their chambers and they lay down to sleep. But from the mountain outside there came a noise that was like moaning forests and falling cataracts. The chamber where each one slept was shaken by the noise. Neither Thor nor Loki nor the lad Thialfi slept that night.

In the morning they left the five-chambered house and turned their faces toward the mountain. It was not a mountain at all, but a Giant. He was lying on the ground when they saw him, but just then he rolled over and sat up. "Little men, little men," he shouted to them, "have you passed by a glove of mine on your way?" He stood up and looked all around him. "Ho, I see my glove now," he said. Thor and Loki and the lad Thialfi stood still as the Giant came toward them. He leaned over and picked up the five-roomed shelter they had slept in. He put it on his hand. It was really his glove!

Thor gripped his hammer, and Loki and the lad Thialfi stood behind him. But the Giant seemed good-humored enough. "Where might ye be bound for, little men?" said he.

"To Utgard in Jötunheim," Thor replied boldly.

"Oh, to that place," said the Giant. "Come, then, I shall be with ye so far. You can call me Skyrmir."

"Can you give us breakfast?" said Thor. He spoke crossly, for he did not want it to appear that there was any reason to be afraid of the Giant.

"I can give you breakfast," said Skyrmir, "but I don't want to stop to eat now. We'll sit down as soon as I have an appetite. Come along now. Here is my wallet to carry. It has my provisions in it."

He gave Thor his wallet. Thor put it on his back and put Thialfi sitting upon it. On and on the Giant strode and Thor and Loki were barely able to keep up with him. It was midday before he showed any signs of halting to take breakfast.

They came to an enormous tree. Under it Skyrmir sat down. "I'll sleep before I eat," he said, "but you can open my wallet, my little men, and make your meal out of it." Saying this, he stretched himself out, and in a few minutes Thor and Loki and the lad Thialfi heard the same sounds as kept them awake the night before, sounds that were like forests moaning and cataracts falling. It was Skyrmir's snoring.

Thor and Loki and the lad Thialfi were too hungry now to be disturbed by these tremendous noises. Thor tried to open the wallet, but he found it was not easy to undo the knots. Then Loki tried to open it. In spite of all Loki's cunning he could not undo the knots. Then Thor took the wallet from him and tried to break the knots by main strength. Not even Thor's strength could break them. He threw the wallet down in his rage.

The snoring of Skyrmir became louder and louder. Thor stood up in his rage. He grasped Miölnir and flung it at the head of the sleeping Giant.

The hammer struck him on the head. But Skyrmir only stirred in his sleep. "Did a leaf fall on my head?" he said.

He turned round on the other side and went to sleep again. The hammer came back to Thor's hand. As soon as Skyrmir snored he flung it again, aiming at the Giant's forehead. It struck there. The Giant opened his eyes. "Has an acorn fallen on my forehead?" he said.

Again he went to sleep. But now Thor, terribly roused, stood over his head with the hammer held in his hands. He struck him on the forehead. It was the greatest blow that Thor had ever dealt.

"A bird is pecking at my forehead—there is no chance to sleep here," said Skyrmir, sitting up. "And you, little men, did you have breakfast yet? Toss over my wallet to me and I shall give you some provision." The lad Thialfi brought him the wallet. Skyrmir opened it, took out his provisions, and gave a share to Thor and Loki and the lad Thialfi. Thor would not take provision from him, but Loki and the lad Thialfi took it and ate. When the meal was finished Skyrmir rose up and said, "Time for us to be going toward Utgard."

As they went on their way Skyrmir talked to Loki. "I always feel very small when I go into Utgard," he said. "You see, I'm such a small and a weak fellow and the folk who live there are so big and powerful. But you and your friends will be welcomed in Utgard. They will be sure to make little pets of you."

And then he left them and they went into Utgard, the City of the Giants. Giants were going up and down in the streets. They were not so huge as Skyrmir would have them believe, Loki noticed.

Utgard was the Asgard of the Giants. But in its buildings there was not a line of the beauty that there was in the palaces of the Gods, Gladsheim and Breidablik or Fensalir. Huge but shapeless the buildings arose, like mountains or icebergs. O beautiful Asgard with the dome above it of the deepest blue! Asgard with the clouds around it heaped up like mountains of diamonds! Asgard with its Rainbow Bridge and its glittering gates! O beautiful Asgard, could it be indeed that these Giants would one day overthrow you?

Thor and Loki with the lad Thialfi went to the palace of the

King. The hammer that Thor gripped would, they knew, make them safe even there. They passed between rows of Giant guards and came to the King's seat. "We know you, Thor and Loki," said the Giant King, "and we know that Thor has come to Utgard to try his strength against the Giants. We shall have a contest to-morrow. To-day there are sports for our boys. If your young servant should like to try his swiftness against our youths, let him enter the race to-day."

Now Thialfi was the best runner in Midgard and all the time he had been with them Loki and Thor had trained him in quickness. And so Thialfi was not fearful of racing against the Giants' youths.

The King called on one named Hugi and placed him against Thialfi. The pair started together. Thialfi sped off. Loki and Thor watched the race anxiously, for they thought it would be well for them if they had a triumph over the dwellers in Utgard in the first contest. But they saw Hugi leave Thialfi behind. They saw the Giant youth reach the winning post, circle round it, and come back to the starting place before Thialfi had reached the end of the course.

Thialfi, who did not know how it was that he had been beaten, asked that he be let run the race with Hugi again. The pair started off once more, and this time it did not seem to Thor and Loki that Hugi had left the starting place at all—he was back there almost as soon as the race had started.

They came back from the racing ground to the palace. The Giant King and his friends with Thor and Loki sat down to the supper table. "To-morrow," said the King, "we shall have our great contest when Asa Thor will show us his power. Have you of Asgard ever heard of one who would enter a contest in eating? We might have a contest in eating at this supper board if we could get one who would match himself with Logi here. He can eat more than anyone in Jötunheim."

"And I," said Loki, "can eat more than any two in Jötunheim. I will match myself against your Logi."

"Good!" said the Giant King. And all the Giants present said, "Good! This will be a sight worth seeing."

Then they put scores of plates along one side of the table, each plate filled with meat. Loki began at one end and Logi began at the other. They started to eat, moving toward each other as each cleared a plate. Plate after plate was emptied, and Thor standing by with the Giants was amazed to see how much Loki ate. But Logi on the other side was leaving plate after plate emptied. At last the two stood together with scores of plates on each side of them. "He has not defeated me," cried Loki. "I have cleared as many plates as your champion, O King of the Giants."

"But you have not cleared them so well," said the King.

"Loki has eaten all the meat that was upon them," said Thor.

"But Logi has eaten the bones with the meat," said the Giant King. "Look and see if it be not so."

Thor went to the plates. Where Loki had eaten, the bones were left on the plates. Where Logi had eaten, nothing was left: bones as well as meat were consumed, and all the plates were left bare.

"We are beaten," said Thor to Loki.

"To-morrow, Thor," said Loki, "you must show all your strength or the Giants will cease to dread the might of the Dwellers in Asgard."

"Be not afraid," said Thor. "No one in Jötunheim will triumph over me."

The next day Thor and Loki came into the great hall of Utgard. The Giant King was there with a throng of his friends. Thor marched into the hall with Miölnir, his great hammer, in his hands. "Our young men have been drinking out of this horn," said the King, "and they want to know if you, Asa Thor, would drink out of it a morning draught. But I must tell you that they think that no one of the Æsir could empty the horn at one draught."

"Give it to me," said Thor. "There is no horn you can hand me that I cannot empty at a draught."

A great horn, brimmed and flowing, was brought over to him. Handing Miölnir to Loki and bidding him stand so that he might keep the hammer in sight, Thor raised the horn to his mouth. He drank and drank. He felt sure there was not a drop left in the horn as he laid it on the ground. "There," he gasped, "your Giant horn is drained."

The Giants looked within the horn and laughed. "Drained, Asa Thor!" said the Giant King. "Look into the horn again. You have hardly drunk below the brim."

And Thor looked into it and saw that the horn was not half emptied. In a mighty rage he lifted it to his lips again. He drank and drank and drank. Then, satisfied that he had emptied it to the bottom, he left the horn on the ground and walked over to the other side of the hall.

"Thor thinks he has drained the horn," said one of the Giants, lifting it up. "But see, friends, what remains in it."

Thor strode back and looked again into the horn. It was still half filled. He turned round to see that all the Giants were laughing at him.

"Asa Thor, Asa Thor," said the Giant King, "we know not how you are going to deal with us in the next feat, but you certainly are not able to drink against the Giants."

Said Thor: "I can lift up and set down any being in your hall."

As he said this a great iron-colored cat bounded into the hall and stood before Thor, her back arched and her fur bristling.

"Then lift the cat off the ground," said the Giant King.

Thor strode to the cat, determined to lift her up and fling her amongst the mocking Giants. He put his hands to the cat, but he could not raise her. Up, up went Thor's arms, up, up, as high as they could go. The cat's arched back went up to the roof, but her feet were never taken off the ground. And as he heaved and heaved with all his might he heard the laughter of the Giants all round him.

He turned away, his eyes flaming with anger. "I am not wont to try to lift cats," he said. "Bring me one to wrestle with, and I swear you shall see me overthrow him."

"Here is one for you to wrestle with, Asa Thor," said the King. Thor looked round and saw an old woman hobbling toward him. She was blear-eyed and toothless. "This is Ellie, my ancient nurse," said the Giant King. "She is the one we would have you wrestle with."

"Thor does not wrestle with old women. I will lay my hands on your tallest Giants instead."

"Ellie has come where you are," said the Giant King. "Now it is she who will lay hands upon you."

The old woman hobbled toward Thor, her eyes gleaming under her falling fringes of gray hair. Thor stood, unable to move as the hag came toward him. She laid her hands upon his arms. Her feet began to trip at his. He tried to cast her from him. Then he found that her feet and her hands were as strong against his as bands and stakes of iron.

Then began a wrestling match in earnest between Thor and the ancient crone Ellie. Round and round the hall they wrestled, and Thor was not able to bend the old woman backward nor sideways. Instead he became less and less able under her terrible grasp. She forced him down, down, and at last he could only save himself from being left prone on the ground by throwing himself down on one knee and holding the hag by the shoulders. She tried to force him down on the ground, but she could not do that. Then she broke from him, hobbled to the door and went out of the hall.

Thor rose up and took the hammer from Loki's hands. Without a word he went out of the hall and along the ways and toward the gate of the Giants' City. He spoke no word to Loki nor to the lad Thialfi who went with him for the seven weeks that they journeyed through Jötunheim.

How Thor and Loki Befooled Thrum the Giant

Loki told another tale about Thor—about Thor and Thrym, a stupid Giant who had cunning streaks in him. Loki and Thor had been in this Giant's house. He had made a feast for them and Thor had been unwatchful.

Then when they were far from Jötunheim Thor missed Miölnir, missed the hammer that was the defence of Asgard and the help of the Gods. He could not remember how or where he had mislaid it. Loki's thoughts went toward Thrym, that stupid Giant who yet had cunning streaks in him. Thor, who had lost the hammer that he had sworn never to let out of his sight, did not know what to do.

But Loki thought it would be worth while to see if Thrym knew anything about it. He went first to Asgard. He hurried across the Rainbow Bridge and passed Heimdall without speaking to him. To none of the Dwellers in Asgard whom he met did he dare relate the tidings of Thor's loss. He spoke to none until he came to Frigga's palace.

To Frigga he said, "You must lend me your falcon dress

until I fly to Thrym's dwelling and find out if he knows where Miölnir is."

"If every feather was silver I would give it to you to go on such an errand," Frigga said.

So Loki put on the falcon dress and flew to Jötunheim and came near Thrym's dwelling. He found the Giant upon a hillside putting golden and silver collars upon the necks of his hounds. Loki in the plumage of a falcon perched on the rock above him, watching the Giant with falcon eyes.

And while he was there he heard the Giant speak boastful words. "I put collars of silver and gold on you now, my hounds," said he, "but soon we Giants will have the gold of Asgard to deck our hounds and our steeds, yea, even the necklace of Freya to put upon you, the best of my hounds. For Miölnir, the defence of Asgard, is in Thrym's holding."

Then Loki spoke to him. "Yea, we know that Miölnir is in thy possession, O Thrym," said he, "but know thou that the eyes of the watchful Gods are upon thee."

"Ha, Loki, Shape-changer," said Thrym, "you are there! But all your watching will not help you to find Miölnir. I have buried Thor's hammer eight miles deep in the earth. Find it if you can. It is below the caves of the Dwarfs."

"It is useless for us to search for Thor's hammer," said Loki; "eh Thrym?"

"It is useless for you to search for it," said the Giant sulkily.

"But what a recompense you would gain if you restored Thor's hammer to the Dwellers in Asgard," Loki said.

"No, cunning Loki, I will never restore it, not for any recompense," said Thrym.

"Yet bethink thee, Thrym," said Loki. "Is there nought in Asgard you would like to own? No treasure, no possession? Odin's ring or Frey's ship, Skidbladnir?"

"No, no," said Thrym. "Only one thing could the Dwellers

in Asgard offer me that I would take in exchange for Miölnir, Thor's hammer."

"And what would that be, Thrym?" said Loki, flying toward him.

"She whom many Giants have striven to gain—Freya, for my wife," said Thrym.

Loki watched Thrym for long with his falcon eyes. He saw that the Giant would not alter his demand. "I will tell the Dwellers in Asgard of your demand," he said at last, and he flew away.

Loki knew that the Dwellers in Asgard would never let Freya be taken from them to become the wife of Thrym, the stupidest of the Giants. He flew back.

By this time all the Dwellers in Asgard had heard of the loss of Miölnir, the help of the Gods. Heimdall shouted to him as he crossed the Rainbow Bridge to ask what tidings he brought back. But Loki did not stop to speak to the Warden of the Bridge but went straight to the hall where the Gods sat in Council.

To the Æsir and the Vanir he told Thrym's demand. None would agree to let the beautiful Freya go live in Jötunheim as a wife to the stupidest of the Giants. All in the Council were cast down. The Gods would never again be able to help mortal men, for now that Miölnir was in the Giants' hands all their strength would have to be used in the defence of Asgard.

So they sat in the Council with looks downcast. But cunning Loki said, "I have thought of a trick that may win back the hammer from stupid Thrym. Let us pretend to send Freya to Jötunheim as a bride for him. But let one of the Gods go in Freya's veil and dress."

"Which of the Gods would bring himself to do so shameful a thing?" said those in the Council.

"Oh, he who lost the hammer, Thor, should be prepared to do as much to win it back," said Loki.

"Thor, Thor! Let Thor win back the hammer from Thrym by Loki's trick," said the Æsir and the Vanir. They left it to Loki to arrange how Thor should go to Jötunheim as a bride for Thrym.

Loki left the Council of the Gods and came to where he had left Thor. "There is but one way to win the hammer back, Thor," he said, "and the Gods in Council have decreed that you shall take it."

"What is the way?" said Thor. "But no matter what it is, tell me of it and I shall do as thou dost say."

"Then," said laughing Loki, "I am to take you to Jötunheim as a bride for Thrym. Thou art to go in bridal dress and veil, in Freya's veil and bridal dress."

"What! I dress in woman's garb?" shouted Thor.

"Yea, Thor, and wear a veil over your head and a garland of flowers upon it."

"I—I wear a garland of flowers?"

"And rings upon thy fingers. And a bunch of housekeeper's keys in thy girdle."

"Cease thy mockery, Loki," said Thor roughly, "or I shall shake thee."

"It is no mockery. Thou wilt have to do this to win Miölnir back for the defence of Asgard. Thrym will take no other recompense than Freya. I would mock him by bringing thee to him in Freya's veil and dress. When thou art in his hall and he asks thee to join hands with him, say thou wilt not until he puts Miölnir into thy hands. Then when thy mighty hammer is in thy holding thou canst deal with him and with all in his hall. And I shall be with thee as thy bridesmaid! O sweet, sweet maiden Thor!"

"Loki," said Thor, "thou didst devise all this to mock me. I in a bridal dress! I with a bride's veil upon me! The Dwellers in Asgard will never cease to laugh at me."

"Yea," said Loki, "but there will never be laughter again in Asgard unless thou art able to bring back the hammer that thine unwatchfulness lost."

"True," said Thor unhappily, "and is this, think'st thou, Loki, the only way to win back Miölnir from Thrym?"

"It is the only way, O Thor," said the cunning Loki.

So Thor and Loki set out for Jötunheim and the dwelling of Thrym. A messenger had gone before them to tell Thrym that Freya was coming with her bridesmaid; that the wedding-feast was to be prepared and the guests gathered and that Miölnir was to be at hand so that it might be given over to the Dwellers in Asgard. Thrym and his Giant mother hastened to have everything in readiness.

Thor and Loki came to the Giant's house in the dress of a bride and a bridesmaid. A veil was over Thor's head hiding his beard and his fierce eyes. A red-embroidered robe he wore and at his side hung a girdle of housekeeper's keys. Loki was veiled, too. The hall of Thrym's greathouse was swept and garnished and great tables were laid for the feast. And Thrym's mother was going from one guest to another, vaunting that her son was getting one of the beauteous Dwellers in Asgard for his bride, Freya, whom so many of the Giants had tried to win.

When Thor and Loki stepped across the threshold Thrym went to welcome them. He wanted to raise the veil of his bride and give her a kiss. Loki quickly laid his hand on the Giant's shoulder.

"Forbear," he whispered. "Do not raise her veil. We Dwellers in Asgard are reserved and bashful. Freya would be much offended to be kissed before this company."

"Aye, aye," said Thrym's old mother. "Do not raise thy bride's veil, son. These Dwellers in Asgard are more refined in their ways than we, the Giants." Then the old woman took Thor by the hand and led him to the table.

The size and the girth of the bride did not surprise the huge Giants who were in the wedding company. They stared at Thor and Loki, but they could see nothing of their faces and little of their forms because of their veils.

Thor sat at the table with Thrym on one side of him and Loki on the other. Then the feast began. Thor, not noticing that what he did was unbecoming to a refined maiden, ate eight salmon right away. Loki nudged him and pressed his foot, but he did not heed Loki. After the salmon he ate a whole ox.

"These maids of Asgard," said the Giants to each other, "they may be refined, as Thrym's mother says, but their appetites are lusty enough."

"No wonder she eats, poor thing," said Loki to Thrym. "It is eight days since we left Asgard. And Freya never ate upon the way, so anxious was she to see Thrym and to come to his house."

"Poor darling, poor darling," said the Giant. "What she has eaten is little after all."

Thor nodded his head toward the mead vat. Thrym ordered his servants to bring a measure to his bride. The servants were kept coming with measures to Thor. While the Giants watched, and while Loki nudged and nodded, he drank three barrels of mead.

"Oh," said the Giants to Thrym's mother, "we are not so sorry that we failed to win a bride from Asgard."

And now a piece of the veil slipped aside and Thor's eyes were seen for an instant. "Oh, how does it come that Freya has such glaring eyes?" said Thrym.

"Poor thing, poor thing," said Loki, "no wonder her eyes are glaring and staring. She has not slept for eight nights, so anxious was she to come to you and to your house, Thrym. But now the time has come for you to join hands with your bride. First, put into her hands the hammer Miölnir that she may know the great recompense that the Giants have given for her coming."

Then Thrym, the stupidest of the Giants, rose up and brought Miölnir, the defence of Asgard, into the feasting hall. Thor could hardly restrain himself from springing up and seizing it from the Giant. But Loki was able to keep him still. Thrym brought over the hammer and put the handle into the hands of her whom he thought was his bride. Thor's hands closed on his hammer. Instantly he stood up. The veil fell off him. His countenance and his blazing eyes were seen by all. He struck one blow on the wall of the house. Down it crashed. Then Thor went striding out of the ruin with Loki beside him, while within the Giants bellowed as the roof and walls fell down on them. And so was Miölnir, the defence of Asgard, lost and won back.

ÆGIR'S FEAST: HOW THOR TRIUMPHED

The time between midday and evening wore on while the Æsir and the Vanir gathered for the feast in old Ægir's hall listened to the stories that Loki told in mockery of Thor. The night came, but no banquet was made ready for the Dwellers in Asgard. They called to Ægir's two underservants, Fimaffenger and Elder, and they bade them bring them a supper. Slight was what they got, but they went to bed saying, "Great must be the preparations that old Ægir is making to feast us to-morrow."

The morrow came and the midday of the morrow, and still the Dwellers in Asgard saw no preparations being made for the banquet. Then Frey rose up and went to seek old Ægir, the Giant King of the Sea. He found him sitting with bowed head in his inner hall. "Ho, Ægir," he said, "what of the banquet that you have offered to the Dwellers in Asgard?"

Old Ægir mumbled and pulled at his beard. At last he looked his guest in the face and told why the banquet was not being made ready. The mead for the feast was not yet brewed. And there was little chance of being able to brew mead that would do for all, for Ægir's hall was lacking a mead kettle that would contain enough.

When the Æsir and the Vanir heard this they were sorely disappointed. Who now, outside of Asgard, would give them a feast? Ægir was the only one of the Giants who was friendly to them, and Ægir could not give them full entertainment.

Then a Giant youth who was there spoke up and said, "My kinsman, the Giant Hrymer, has a mead kettle that is a mile wide. If we could bring Hrymer's kettle here, what a feast we might have!"

"One of us can go for that kettle," Frey said.

"Ah, but Hrymer's dwelling is beyond the deepest forest and behind the highest mountain," the Giant youth said, "and Hrymer himself is a rough and a churlish one to call on."

"Still, one of us should go," Frey said.

"I will go to Hrymer's dwelling," said Thor, standing up. "I will go to Hrymer's dwelling and get the mile-wide kettle from him by force or cunning." He had been sitting subdued under the mocking tales that Loki told of him and he was pleased with this chance to make his prowess plain to the Æsir and the Vanir. He buckled on the belt that doubled his strength. He drew on the iron gloves that enabled him to grasp Miölnir. He took his hammer in his hands, and he signed to the Giant youth to come with him and be his guide.

The Æsir and the Vanir applauded Thor as he stepped out of old Ægir's hall. But Loki, mischievous Loki, threw a gibe after him. "Do not let the hammer out of your hands this time, bride of Thrym," he shouted.

Thor, with the Giant youth to guide him, went through the deepest forest and over the highest mountain. He came at last to the Giant's dwelling. On a hillock before Hrymer's house was a dreadful warden; a Giant crone she was, with heads a-many growing out of her shoulders. She was squatting down on her ankles, and her heads, growing in bunches, were looking in different directions. As Thor and the Giant youth came near screams and yelps came from all her heads. Thor grasped his hammer and would have flung it at her if a Giant woman, making a sign of peace, had not come to the door of the dwelling. The youthful Giant who was with Thor greeted her as his mother.

"Son, come within," said she, "and you may bring your fellow farer with you."

The Giant crone—she was Hrymer's grandmother—kept up her screaming and yelping. But Thor went past her and into the Giant's dwelling.

When she saw that it was one of the Dwellers in Asgard who had come with her son the Giant woman grew fearful for them both. "Hrymer," she said, "will be in a rage to find one of the Æsir under his roof. He will strive to slay you."

"It is not likely he will succeed," Thor said, grasping Miölnir, the hammer that all the Giant race knew of and dreaded.

"Hide from him," said the Giant woman. "He may injure my son in his rage to find you here."

"I am not wont to hide from the Giants," Thor said.

"Hide only for a little while! Hide until Hrymer has eaten," the Giant woman pleaded. "He comes back from the chase in a stormy temper. After he has eaten he is easier to deal with. Hide until he has finished supper."

Thor at last agreed to do this. He and the Giant youth hid behind a pillar in the hall. They were barely hidden when they heard the clatter of the Giant's steps as he came through the court-yard. He came to the door. His beard was like a frozen forest around his mouth. And he dragged along with him a wild bull that he had captured in the chase. So proud was he of his capture that he dragged it into the hall.

"I have taken alive," he shouted, "the bull with the mightiest head and horns. 'Heaven-breaking' this bull is called. No Giant but me could capture it." He tied the bull to the post of the door and then his eyes went toward the pillar behind which Thor and the Giant youth were hiding. The pillar split up its whole length at that look from Hrymer's eyes. He came nearer. The pillar of stone broke across. It fell with the cross-beam it supported and all the kettles and cauldrons that were hanging on the beam came down with a terrible rattle.

Then Thor stepped out and faced the wrathful Giant. "It is I who am here, friend Hrymer," he said, his hands resting on his hammer.

Then Hrymer, who knew Thor and knew the force of Thor's hammer, drew back. "Now that you are in my house, Asa Thor," he said, "I will not quarrel with you. Make supper ready for Asa Thor and your son and myself," said he to the Giant woman.

A plentiful supper was spread and Hrymer and Thor and the Giant youth sat down to three whole roast oxen. Thor ate the whole of one ox. Hrymer, who had eaten nearly two himself, leaving only small cuts for his wife and his youthful kinsman, grumbled at Thor's appetite. "You'll clear my fields, Asa Thor," he said, "if you stay long with me."

"Do not grumble, Hrymer," Thor said. "To-morrow I'll go fishing and I'll bring you back the weight of what I ate."

"Then instead of hunting I'll go fishing with you to-morrow, Asa Thor," said Hrymer. "And don't be frightened if I take you out on a rough sea."

Hrymer was first out of bed the next morning. He came with the pole and the ropes in his hand to where Thor was sleeping.

"Time to start earning your meal, Asa Thor," said he.

Thor got out of bed, and when they were both in the court-yard the Giant said, "You'll have to provide a bait for yourself.

Mind that you take a bait large enough. It is not where the little fishes are, the place where I'm going to take you. If you never saw monsters before you'll see them now. I'm glad, Asa Thor, that you spoke of going fishing."

"Will this bait be big enough?" said Thor, laying his hands on the horns of the bull that Hrymer had captured and brought home, the bull with the mighty head of horns that was called "Heaven-breaking." "Will this bait be big enough, do you think?"

"Yes, if you're big enough to handle it," said the Giant.

Thor said nothing, but he struck the bull full in the middle of the forehead with his fist. The great creature fell down dead. Thor then twisted the bull's head off. "I have my bait and I'm ready to go with you, Hrymer," he said.

Hrymer had turned away to hide the rage he was in at seeing Thor do such a feat. He walked down to the boat without speaking. "You may row for the first few strokes," said Hrymer, when they were in the boat, "but when we come to where the ocean is rough, why I'll take the oars from you."

Without saying a word Thor made a few strokes that took the boat out into the middle of the ocean. Hrymer was in a rage to think that he could not show himself greater than Thor. He let out his line and began to fish. Soon he felt something huge on his hook. The boat rocked and rocked till Thor steadied it. Then Hrymer drew into the boat the largest whale that was in these seas.

Good fishing," said Thor, as he put his own bait on the line.

"It's something for you to tell the Æsir," said Hrymer."I thought as you were here I'd show you something bigger than salmon-fishing."

"I'll try my luck now," said Thor.

He threw out a line that had at the end of it the mighty-horned head of the great bull. Down, down the head went. It passed where the whales swim, and the whales were afraid to gulp at the mighty horns. Down, down it went till it came near where the monster serpent that coils itself round the world abides. It reared its head up from its serpent coils as Thor's bait came down through the depths of the ocean. It gulped at the head and drew it into its gullet. There the great hook stuck. Terribly surprised was the serpent monster. It lashed the ocean into a fury. But still the hook stayed. Then it strove to draw down to the depths of the ocean the boat of those who had hooked it. Thor put his legs across the boat and stretched them till they touched the bottom bed of the ocean. On the bottom bed of the ocean Thor stood and he pulled and he pulled on his line. The serpent monster lashed the ocean into fiercer and fiercer storms and all the world's ships were hurled against each other and wrecked and tossed. But it had to loosen coil after coil of the coils it makes around the world. Thor pulled and pulled. Then the terrible head of the serpent monster appeared above the waters. It reared over the boat that Hrymer sat in and that Thor straddled across. Thor dropped the line and took up Miölnir, his mighty hammer. He raised it to strike the head of the serpent monster whose coils go round the world. But Hrymer would not have that happen. Rather than have Thor pass him by such a feat he cut the line, and the head of the serpent monster sank back into the sea. Thor's hammer was raised. He hurled it, hurled that hammer that always came back to his hand. It followed the sinking head through fathom after fathom of the ocean depth. It struck the serpent monster a blow, but not such a deadly blow as would have been struck if the water had not come between. A bellow of pain came up from the depths of the ocean, such a bellow of pain that all in Jötunheim were affrighted.

"This surely is something to tell the Æsir of," said Thor, "something to make them forget Loki's mockeries."

Without speaking Hrymer turned the boat and rowed toward the shore, dragging the whale in the wake. He was in such a rage to think that one of the Æsir had done a feat surpassing his that he would not speak. At supper, too, he remained silent, but Thor talked for two, boasting loudly of his triumph over the monster serpent.

"No doubt you think yourself very powerful, Asa Thor," Hrymer said at last. "Well, do you think you are powerful enough to break the cup that is before you?"

Thor took up the cup and with a laugh he hurled it against the stone pillar of the house. The cup fell down on the floor without a crack or a dint in it. But the pillar was shattered with the blow.

The Giant laughed. "So feeble are the folk of Asgard!" he said.

Thor took up the cup again and flung it with greater force against the stone pillar. And again the cup fell to the ground without a crack or a dint.

Then he heard the woman who was the mother of the Giant youth sing softly, as she plied her wheel behind him:

Not at the pillar of the stead,
But at Hrymer's massy head:
When you next the goblet throw,
Let his head receive the blow.

Thor took the cup up again. He flung it, not at the pillar this time, but at Hrymer's head. It struck the Giant full on the forehead and fell down on the floor in pieces. And Hrymer's head was left without a dint or a crack.

"Ha, so you can break a cup, but can you lift up my mile-wide kettle?" cried the Giant.

"Show me where your mile-wide kettle is and I shall try to lift it," cried Thor.

The Giant took up the flooring and showed him the mile-wide kettle down in the cellar. Thor stooped down and took the kettle by the brim. He lifted it slowly as if with a mighty effort.

"You can lift, but can you carry it?" said the Giant.

"I will try to do that," said Thor. He lifted the kettle up and placed it on his head. He strode to the door and out of the house before the Giant could lay hands on him. Then when he was outside he started to run. He was across the mountain before he looked behind him. He heard a yelping and a screaming and he saw the Giant crone with the bunch of heads running, running after him. Up hill and down dale Thor raced, the mile-wide kettle on his head and the Giant crone in chase of him. Through the deep forest he ran and over the high mountain, but still Bunch-of-Heads kept him in chase. But at last, jumping over a lake, she fell in and Thor was free of his pursuer.

And so back to the Æsir and the Vanir Thor came in triumph, carrying on his head the mile-wide kettle. And those of the Æsir and the Vanir who had laughed most at Loki's mockeries rose up and cheered for him as he came in. The mead was brewed, the feast was spread, and the greatest banquet that ever the Kings of the Giants gave to the Dwellers in Asgard was eaten in gladness.

A strange and silent figure sat at the banquet. It was the figure of a Giant and no one knew who he was nor where he had come from. But when the banquet was ended Odin, the Eldest of the Gods, turned toward this figure and said, "O Skyrmir, Giant King of Utgard, rise up now and tell Thor of all you practiced upon him when he and Loki came to your City."

Then the stranger at the banquet stood up, and Thor and

Loki saw he was the Giant King in whose halls they had had the contests. Skyrmir turned toward them and said:

"O Thor and O Loki, I will reveal to you now the deceits I practiced on you both. It was I whom ye met on the moorland on the day before ye came into Utgard. I gave you my name as Skyrmir and I did all I might do to prevent your entering our City, for the Giants dreaded a contest of strength with Asa Thor. Now hear me, O Thor. The wallet I gave for you to take provisions out of was tied with magic knots. No one could undo them by strength or cleverness. And while you were striving to undo them I placed a mountain of rock between myself and you. The hammer blows, which as you thought struck me, struck the mountain and made great clefts and gaps in it. When I knew the strength of your tremendous blows I was more and more in dread of your coming into our City.

"I saw you would have to be deceived by magic. Your lad Thialfi was the one whom I first deceived. For it was not a Giant youth who raced against him, but Thought itself. And even you, O Loki, I deceived. For when you tried to make your-self out the greatest of eaters I pitted against you, not a Giant, but Fire that devours everything.

"You, Thor, were deceived in all the contests. After you had taken the drinking horn in your hands we were all affrighted to see how much you were able to gulp down. For the end of that horn was in the sea, and Ægir, who is here, can tell you that after you had drunk from it, the level of the sea went down.

"The cat whom you strove to lift was Nidhögg, the dragon that gnaws at the roots of Ygdrassil, the Tree of Trees. Truly we were terrified when we saw that you made Nidhögg budge. When you made the back of the cat reach the roof of our palace we said to ourselves, 'Thor is the mightiest of all the beings we have known.'

"Lastly you strove with the hag Ellie. Her strength seemed

marvelous to you, and you thought yourself disgraced because you could not throw her. But know, Thor, that Ellie whom you wrestled with was Old Age herself. We were terrified again to see that she who can overthrow all was not able to force you prone upon the ground."

So Skyrmir spoke and then left the hall. And once more the Æsir and the Vanir stood up and cheered for Thor, the strongest of all who guarded Asgard.

THE DWARF'S HOARD, AND THE CURSE THAT IT BROUGHT

Now old Ægir's feast was over and all the Æsir and the Vanir made ready for their return to Asgard. Two only went on another way—Odin, the Eldest of the Gods, and Loki the Mischievous.

Loki and Odin laid aside all that they had kept of the divine power and the divine strength. They were going into the World of Men, and they would be as men merely. Together they went through Midgard, mingling with men of all sorts, kings and farmers, outlaws and true men, warriors and householders, thralls and councillors, courteous men and men who were ill-mannered. One day they came to the bank of a mighty river and there they rested, listening to the beat of iron upon iron in a place near by.

Presently, on a rock in the middle of the river, they saw an otter come. The otter went into the water and came back to the rock with a catch of salmon. He devoured it there. Then Odin saw Loki do a senseless and an evil thing. Taking up a great stone he flung it at the otter. The stone struck the beast on the skull and knocked him over dead.

"Loki, Loki, why hast thou done a thing so senseless and so evil?" Odin said. Loki only laughed. He swam across the water and came back with the creature of the river. "Why didst thou take the life of the beast?" Odin said.

"The mischief in me made me do it," said Loki. He drew out his knife and ripping the otter up he began to flay him. When the skin was off the beast he folded it up and stuck it in his belt. Then Odin and he left that place by the river.

They came to a house with two smithies beside it, and from the smithies came the sound of iron beating upon iron. They went within the house and they asked that they might eat there and rest themselves.

An old man who was cooking fish over a fire pointed out a bench to them. "Rest there," said he, "and when the fish is cooked I will give you something good to eat. My son is a fine fisher and he brings me salmon of the best."

Odin and Loki sat on the bench and the old man went on with his cooking. "My name is Hreidmar," he said, "and I have two sons who work in the smithies without. I have a third son also. It is he who does the fishing for us. And who may ye be, O wayfaring men?"

Loki and Odin gave names to Hreidmar that were not the names by which they were known in Asgard or on Midgard. Hreidmar served fish to them and they ate. "And what adventures have ye met upon your travels?" Hreidmar asked. "Few folk come this way to tell me of happenings."

"I killed an otter with a cast of a stone," Loki said with a laugh.

"You killed an otter!" Hreidmar cried. "Where did you kill one?"

"Where I killed him is of no import to you, old man," said Loki. "His skin is a good one, however. I have it at my belt."

Hreidmar snatched the skin out of Loki's belt. As soon as he held the skin before his eyes he shrieked out, "Fafnir, Regin, my sons, come here and bring the thralls of your smithies. Come, come, come!"

"Why dost thou make such an outcry, old man?" said Odin.

"Ye have slain my son Otter," shrieked the old man. "This in my hands is the skin of my son."

As Hreidmar said these two young men bearing the forehammers of them smithies came in followed by the thralls. "Strike these men dead with your forehammers, O Fafnir, O Regin," their father cried. "Otter, who used to stay in the river, and whom I changed by enchantment into a river beast that he might fish for me, has been slain by these men."

"Peace," said Odin. "We have slain thy son, it would seem, but it was unwittingly that we did the deed. We will give a recompense for the death of thy son."

"What recompense will ye give?" said Hreidmar, looking at Odin with eyes that were small and sharp.

Then did Odin, the Eldest of the Gods, say a word that was unworthy of his wisdom and his power. He might have said, "I will bring thee a draught of Mimir's well water as a recompense for thy son's death." But instead of thinking of wisdom, Odin All-Father thought of gold. "Set a price on the life of thy son and we will pay that price in gold," he said.

"Maybe ye are great kings traveling through the world," Hreidmar said. "If ye are ye will have to find gold that will cover every hair upon the skin of him whom ye have killed."

Then did Odin, his mind being fixed upon the gold, think upon a certain treasure, a treasure that was guarded by a Dwarf. No other treasure in the nine worlds would be great enough to make the recompense that Hreidmar claimed. He thought upon this treasure and he thought on how it might be taken and yet he was ashamed of his thought.

"Dost thou, Loki, know of Andvari's hoard?" he said.

"I know of it," said Loki sharply, "and I know where it is hidden. Wilt thou, Odin, win leave for me to fetch Andvari's hoard?"

Odin spoke to Hreidmar. "I will stay with thee as a hostage," he said, "if thou wilt let this one go to fetch a treasure that will cover the otter's skin hair by hair."

"I will let this be done," said old Hreidmar with the sharp and cunning eyes. "Go now," said he to Loki. Then Loki went from the house.

Andvari was a Dwarf who, in the early days, had gained for himself the greatest treasure in the nine worlds. So that he might guard this treasure unceasingly he changed himself into a fish—into a pike—and he swam in the water before the cave where the hoard was hidden.

All in Asgard knew of the Dwarf and of the hoard he guarded. And there was a thought amongst all that this hoard was not to be meddled with and that some evil was joined to it. But now Odin had given the word that it was to be taken from the Dwarf. Loki set out for Andvari's cave rejoicingly. He came to the pool before the cave and he watched for a sight of Andvari. Soon he saw the pike swimming cautiously before the cave.

He would have to catch the pike and hold him till the treasure was given for ransom. As he watched the pike became aware of him. Suddenly he flung himself forward in the water and went with speed down the stream.

Not with his hands and not with any hook and line could Loki catch that pike. How, then, could he take him? Only with a net that was woven by magic. Then Loki thought of where he might get such a net.

Ran, the wife of old Ægir, the Giant King of the Sea, had a net that was woven by magic. In it she took all that was wrecked on the sea. Loki thought of Ran's net and he turned and went back to Ægir's hall to ask for the Queen. But Ran was seldom in her husband's dwelling. She was now down by the rocks of the sea.

He found Ran, the cold Queen, standing in the flow of the sea, drawing out of the depths with the net that she held in her hands every piece of treasure that was washed that way. She had made a heap of the things she had drawn out of the sea, corals and amber, and bits of gold and silver, but still she was plying her net greedily.

"Thou knowest me, Ægir's wife," said Loki to her.

"I know thee, Loki," said Queen Ran.

"Lend me thy net," said Loki.

"That I will not do," said Queen Ran.

"Lend me thy net that I may catch Andvari the Dwarf who boasts that he has a greater treasure than ever thou wilt take out of the sea," said Loki.

The cold Queen of the sea ceased plying her net. She looked at Loki steadily. Yes, if he were going to catch Andvari she would lend her net to him. She hated all the Dwarfs because this one and that one had told her they had greater treasures than ever she would be mistress of. But especially she hated Andvari, the Dwarf who had the greatest treasure in the nine worlds.

"There is nothing more to gather here," she said, "and if thou wilt swear to bring me back my net by to-morrow I shall lend it to you."

"I swear by the sparks of Muspelheim that I will bring thy net back to thee by to-morrow, O Queen of Ægir," Loki cried. Then Ran put into his hands the Magic Net. Back then he went to where the Dwarf, transformed, was guarding his wondrous hoard.

Dark was the pool in which Andvari floated as a pike; dark it was, but to him it was all golden with the light of his wondrous treasure. For the sake of this hoard he had given up his companionship with the Dwarfs and his delight in making and shaping the things of their workmanship. For the sake of his hoard he had taken on himself the dumbness and deafness of a fish.

Now as he swam about before the cave he was aware again of a shadow above him. He slipped toward the shadow of the bank. Then as he turned round he saw a net sweeping toward him. He sank down in the water. But the Magic Net had spread out and he sank into its meshes.

Suddenly he was out of the water and was left gasping on the bank. He would have died had he not undone his transformation.

Soon he appeared as a Dwarf. "Andvari, you are caught; it is one of the Æsir who has taken you," he heard his captor say.

"Loki," he gasped.

"Thou art caught and thou shalt be held," Loki said to him. "It is the will of the Æsir that thou give up thy hoard to me."

"My hoard, my hoard!" the Dwarf shouted. "Never will I give up my hoard."

"I hold thee till thou givest it to me," said Loki.

"Unjust, unjust," shouted Andvari. "It is only thou, Loki, who art unjust. I will go to the throne of Odin and I will have Odin punish thee for striving to rob me of my treasure."

"Odin has sent me to fetch thy hoard to him," said Loki.

"Can it be that all the Æsir are unjust? Ah, yes. In the beginning of things they cheated the Giant who built the wall round their City. The Æsir are unjust."

Loki had Andvari in his power. And after the Dwarf had raged against him and defied him, he tormented him; at last, trembling with rage and with his face covered with tears, Andvari took Loki into his cavern, and, turning a rock aside, showed him the mass of gold and gems that was his hoard.

At once Loki began to gather into the Magic Net lumps and ingots and circlets of gold with gems that were rubies and sapphires and emeralds. He saw Andvari snatch at something on the heap, but he made no sign of marking it. At last all was gathered into the net, and Loki stood there ready to bear the Dwarf's hoard away.

"There is one thing more to be given," said Loki, "the ring that you, Andvari, snatched from the heap."

"I snatched nothing," said the Dwarf. But he shook with anger and his teeth gnashed together and froth came on his lips. "I snatched nothing from the heap."

But Loki pulled up his arm and there fell to the ground the ring that Andvari had hidden under his armpit.

It was the most precious thing in all the hoard. Had it been left with him Andvari would have thought that he still possessed a treasure, for this ring of itself could make gold. It was made out of gold that was refined of all impurities and it was engraven with a rune of power.

Loki took up this most precious ring and put it on his finger. Then the Dwarf screamed at him, turning his thumbs toward him in a curse:

> The ring with the rune
> Of power upon it:
> May it weigh down your fortune,
> And load you with evil,
> You, Loki, and all
> Who lust to possess
> The ring I have cherished.

As Andvari uttered this curse Loki saw a figure rise up in the cave and move toward him. As this figure came near he knew who it was: Gulveig, a Giant woman who had once been in Asgard.

Far back in the early days, when the Gods had come to their holy hill and before Asgard was built, three women of the Giants had come amongst the Æsir. After the Three had been with them for a time, the lives of the Æsir changed. Then did they begin to value and to hoard the gold that they had played with. Then did they think of war. Odin hurled his spear amongst the messengers that came from the Vanir, and war came into the world.

The Three were driven out of Asgard. Peace was made with the Vanir. The Apples of Lasting Youth were grown in Asgard. The eagerness for gold was curbed. But never again were the Æsir as happy as they were before the women came to them from the Giants.

Gulveig was one of the Three who had blighted the early happiness of the Gods. And, behold, she was in the cave where Andvari had hoarded his treasure and with a smile upon her face she was advancing toward Loki.

"So, Loki," she said, "thou seest me again. And Odin who sent thee to this cave will see me again. Lo, Loki! I go to Odin to be thy messenger and to tell him that thou comest with Andvari's hoard."

And speaking so, and smiling into his face, Gulveig went out of the cave with swift and light steps. Loki drew the ends of the Magic Net together and gathering all the treasures in its meshes he, too, went out.

Odin, the Eldest of the Gods, stood leaning on his spear and looking at the skin of the otter that was spread out before him. One came into the dwelling swiftly. Odin looked and saw that she who had come in on such swift, glad feet was Gulveig who, once with her two companions, had troubled the happiness of the Gods. Odin raised his spear to cast it at her.

"Lay thy spear down, Odin," she said. "I dwelt for long in the Dwarf's cave. But thy word unloosed me, and the curse said over Andvari's ring has sent me here. Lay thy spear down, and look on me, O Eldest of the Gods.

"Thou didst cast me out of Asgard, but thy word has brought me to come back to thee. And if ye two, Odin and Loki, have bought yourselves free with gold and may enter Asgard, surely I, Gulveig, am free to enter Asgard also."

Odin lowered his spear, sighing deeply. "Surely it is so, Gulveig," he said. "I may not forbid thee to enter Asgard. Would I had thought of giving the man Kvasir's Mead or Mimir's well water rather than this gold as a recompense."

As they spoke Loki came into Hreidmar's dwelling. He laid on the floor the Magic Net. Old Hreidmar with his sharp eyes, and huge Fafnir, and lean and hungry-looking Regin came in to gaze on the gold and gems that shone through the meshes. They began to push each other away from gazing at the gold. Then Hreidmar cried out, "No one may be here but these two kings and I while we measure out the gold and gems and see whether the recompense be sufficient. Go without, go without, sons of mine."

Then Fafnir and Regin were forced to go out of the dwelling. They went out slowly, and Gulveig went with them, whispering to both. With shaking hands old Hreidmar spread out the skin that once covered his son. He drew out the ears and the tail and the paws so that every single hair could be shown. For long he was on his hands and knees, his sharp eyes searching, searching over every line of the skin. And still on his knees he said, "Begin now, O kings, and cover with a gem or a piece of gold every hair on the skin that was my son's."

Odin stood leaning on his spear, watching the gold and gems being paid out. Loki took the gold—the ingots, and the lumps and the circlets; he took the gems—the rubies, and the emeralds and the sapphires, and he began to place them over each hair. Soon the middle of the skin was all covered. Then he put the gems and the gold over the paws and the tail. Soon the otter-skin was so glittering that one would think it could light up the world. And still Loki went on finding a place where a gem or a piece of gold might be put.

At last he stood up. Every gem and every piece of gold had been taken out of the net. And every hair on the otter's skin had been covered with a gem or a piece of gold.

And still old Hreidmar on his hands and knees was peering over the skin, searching, searching for a hair that was not covered. At last he lifted himself up on his knees. His mouth was open, but he was speechless. He touched Odin on the knees, and when Odin bent down he showed him a hair upon the lip that was left uncovered.

"What meanest thou?" Loki cried, turning upon the crouching man.

"Your ransom is not paid yet—look, here is still a hair uncovered. You may not go until every hair is covered with gold or a gem."

"Peace, old man," said Loki roughly. "All the Dwarf's hoard has been given thee."

"Ye may not go until every hair has been covered," Hreidmar said again.

"There is no more gold or gems," Loki answered.

"Then ye may not go," cried Hreidmar, springing up.

It was true. Odin and Loki might not leave that dwelling until the recompense they had agreed to was paid in full. Where now would the Æsir go for gold?

And then Odin saw the gleam of gold on Loki's finger: it was the ring he had forced from Andvari. "Thy finger-ring," said Odin. "Put thy finger-ring over the hair on the otter's skin."

Loki took off the ring that was engraved with the rune of power, and he put it on the lip-hair of the otter's skin. Then Hreidmar clapped his hands and screamed aloud. Huge Fafnir and lean and hungry-looking Regin came within, and Gulveig came behind them. They stood around the skin of the son and the brother that was all glittering with gold and gems. But they looked at each other more than they looked on the glittering mass, and very deadly were the looks that Fafnir and Regin cast upon their father and cast upon each other.

Over Bifröst, the Rainbow Bridge, went all of the Æsir and the Vanir that had been at old Ægir's feast—Frey and Freya, Frigga, Iduna, and Sif; Tyr with his sword and Thor in his chariot drawn by the goats. Loki came behind them, and behind them all came Odin, the Father of the Gods. He went slowly with his head bent, for he knew that an unwelcome one was following—Gulveig, who once had been cast out of Asgard and whose return now the Gods might not gain say.

PART THREE
THE WITCH'S HEART

FOREBODING IN ASGARD

What happened afterwards is to the shame of the Gods, and mortals may hardly speak of it. Gulveig the Witch came into Asgard, for Heimdall might not forbid her entrance. She came within and she had her seat amongst the Æsir and the Vanir. She walked through Asgard with a smile upon her face, and where she walked and where she smiled Care and dire Foreboding came.

Those who felt the care and the foreboding most deeply were Bragi the Poet and his wife, the fair and simple Iduna, she who gathered the apples that kept age from the Dwellers in Asgard. Bragi ceased to tell his never-ending tale. Then one day, overcome by the fear and the foreboding that was creeping through Asgard, Iduna slipped down Ygdrassil, the World Tree, and no one was left to pluck the apples with which the Æsir and the Vanir stayed their youth.

Then were all the Dwellers in Asgard in sore dismay. Strength and beauty began to fade from all. Thor found it hard to lift Miölnir, his great hammer, and the flesh under Freya's necklace lost its white radiance. And still Gulveig the Witch walked smiling through Asgard, although now she was hated by all.

It was Odin and Frey who went in search of Iduna. She would have been found and brought back without delay if Frey had had with him the magic sword that he had bartered for Gerda. In his search he had to strive with one who guarded the lake wherein Iduna had hidden herself. Beli was the one he strove against. He overcame him in the end with a weapon made of stags' antlers. Ah, it was not then but later that Frey lamented the loss of his sword: it was when the Riders of Muspell came against Asgard, and the Vanir, who might have prevailed, prevailed not because of the loss of Frey's sword.

They found Iduna and they brought her back. But still Care and Foreboding crept through Asgard. And it was known, too, that the witch Gulveig was changing the thoughts of the Gods.

At last Odin had to judge Gulveig. He judged her and decreed her death. And only Gungnir, the spear of Odin, might slay Gulveig, who was not of mortal race.

Odin hurled Gungnir. The spear went through Gulveig. But still she stood smiling at the Gods. A second time Odin hurled his spear. A second time Gungnir pierced the witch. She stood livid as one dead but fell not down. A third time Odin hurled his spear. And now, pierced for the third time, the witch gave a scream that made all Asgard shudder and she fell in death on the ground.

"I have slain in these halls where slaying is forbidden," Odin said. "Take now the corpse of Gulveig and burn it on the ramparts, so that no trace of the witch who has troubled us will remain in Asgard."

They brought the corpse of Gulveig the witch out on the ramparts and they lighted fires under the pile on which they laid her and they called upon Hræsvelgur to fan up the flame:

Hræsvelgur is the Giant,
Who on heaven's edge sits
In the guise of an eagle;
And the winds, it is said,
Rush down on the earth
From his outspreading pinions.

Far away was Loki when all this was being done. Often now he went from Asgard, and his journeys were to look upon that wondrous treasure that had passed from the keeping of the Dwarf Andvari. It was Gulveig who had kept the imagination of that treasure within his mind. Now, when he came back and heard the whispers of what had been done, a rage flamed up within him. For Loki was one of those whose minds were being changed by the presence and the whispers of the witch Gulveig. His mind was being changed to hatred of the Gods. Now he went to the place of Gulveig's burning. All her body was in ashes, but her heart had not been devoured by the flames. And Loki in his rage took the heart of the witch and ate it. Oh, black and direful was it in Asgard, the day that Loki ate the heart that the flames would not devour!

LOKI THE BETRAYER

He stole Frigga's dress of falcon feathers. Then as a falcon he flew out of Asgard. Jötunheim was the place that he flew toward.

The anger and the fierceness of the hawk was within Loki as he flew through the Giants' Realm. The heights and the chasms of that dread land made his spirits mount up like fire. He saw the whirlpools and the smoking mountains and had joy of these sights. Higher and higher he soared until, looking toward the South, he saw the flaming land of Muspelheim. Higher and higher still he soared. With his falcon's eyes he saw the gleam of Surtur's flaming sword. All the fire of Muspelheim and all the gloom of Jötunheim would one day be brought against Asgard and against Midgard. But Loki was no longer dismayed to think of the ruin of Asgard's beauty and the ruin of Midgard's promise.

He hovered around one of the dwellings in Jötunheim. Why had he come to it? Because he had seen two of the women of that dwelling, and his rage against the Asyniur and the Vanir was such that the ugliness and the evil of these women was pleasing to him.

He hovered before the open door of the Giant's house and he looked upon those who were within. Gerriöd, the most savage of all the Giants, was there. And beside him, squatting on the ground, were his two evil and ugly daughters, Gialp and Greip.

They were big and bulky, black and rugged, with horses' teeth and hair that was like horses' manes. Gialp was the uglier of the two, if one could be said to be uglier than the other, for her nose was a yard long and her eyes were crooked.

What were they talking about as they sat there, one scratching the other? Of Asgard and the Dwellers in Asgard whom they hated. Thor was the one whom they hated most of all, and they were speaking of all they would like to do to him.

"I would keep Thor bound in chains," said Gerriöd the Giant, "and I would beat him to death with my iron club."

"I would grind his bones to powder," said Greip.

"I would tear the flesh off his bones," said Gialp. "Father, can you not catch this Thor and bring him to us alive?"

"Not so long as he has his hammer Miölnir, and the gloves with which he grasps his hammer, and the belt that doubles his strength."

Oh, if we could catch him without his hammer and his belt and his gloves," cried Gialp and Greip together.

At that moment they saw the falcon hovering before the door. They were eager now for something to hold and torment and so the hearts of the three became set upon catching the falcon. They did not stir from the place where they were sitting, but they called the child Glapp, who was swinging from the roof-tree, and they bade him go out and try to catch the falcon.

All concealed by the great leaves the child Glapp climbed

up the ivy that was around the door. The falcon came hovering near. Then Glapp caught it by the wings and fell down through the ivy, screaming and struggling as he was being beaten, and clawed, and torn by the wings and the talons and the beak of the falcon.

Gerriöd and Greip and Gialp rushed out and kept hold of the falcon. As the Giant held him in his hands and looked him over he knew that this was no bird-creature. The eyes showed him to be of Alfheim or Asgard. The Giant took him and shut him in a box till he would speak.

Soon he tapped at the closed box and when Gerriöd opened it Loki spoke to him. So glad was the savage Giant to have one of the Dwellers in Asgard in his power that he and his daughters did nothing but laugh and chuckle to each other for days. And all this time they left Loki in the closed box to waste with hunger.

When they opened the box again Loki spoke to them. He told them he would do any injury to the Dwellers in Asgard that would please them if they would let him go.

"Will you bring Thor to us?" said Greip.

"Will you bring Thor to us without his hammer, and without the gloves with which he grasps his hammer, and without his belt?" said Gialp.

"I will bring him to you if you will let me go," Loki said. "Thor is easily deceived and I can bring him to you without his hammer and his belt and his gloves."

"We will let you go, Loki," said the Giant, "if you will swear by the gloom of Jötunheim that you will bring Thor to us as you say."

Loki swore that he would do so by the gloom of Jötunheim —"Yea, and by the fires of Muspelheim," he added. The Giant and his daughters let him go, and he flew back to Asgard.

He restored to Frigga her falcon dress. All blamed him for

having stolen it, but when he told how he had been shut up without food in Gerriöd's dwelling those who judged him thought he had been punished enough for the theft. He spoke as before to the Dwellers in Asgard, and the rage and hatred he had against them since he had eaten Gulveig's heart he kept from bursting forth.

He talked to Thor of the adventures they had together in Jötunheim. Thor would now roar with laughter when he talked of the time when he went as a bride to Thrym the Giant.

Loki was able to persuade him to make another journey to Jötunheim. "And I want to speak to you of what I saw in Gerriöd's dwelling," he said. "I saw there the hair of Sif, your wife."

"The hair of Sif, my wife," said Thor in surprise.

"Yes, the hair I once cut off from Sif's head," said Loki. "Gerriöd was the one who found it when I cast it away. They light their hall with Sif's hair. Oh, yes, they don't need torches where Sif's hair is."

"I should like to see it," said Thor.

"Then pay Gerriöd a visit," Loki replied. "But if you go to his house you will have to go without your hammer Miölnir, and without your gloves and your belt."

"Where will I leave Miölnir, and my gloves and my belt?" Thor asked.

"Leave them in Valaskjalf, Odin's own dwelling," said cunning Loki.

"Leave them there and come to Gerriöd's dwelling. Surely you will be well treated there."

"Yes, I will leave them in Valaskjalf and go with you to Gerriöd's dwelling," Thor said.

Thor left his hammer, his gloves, and his belt in Valaskjalf. Then he and Loki went toward Jötunheim. When they were near the end of their journey, they came to a wide river, and with a young Giant whom they met on the bank they began to ford it.

Suddenly the river began to rise. Loki and the young Giant would have been swept away only Thor gripped both of them. Higher and higher the river rose, and rougher and rougher it became. Thor had to plant his feet firmly on the bottom or he and the two he held would have been swept down by the flood. He struggled across, holding Loki and the young Giant. A mountain ash grew out of the bank, and, while the two held to him, he grasped it with his hands. The river rose still higher, but Thor was able to draw Loki and the young Giant to the bank, and then he himself scrambled up on it.

Now looking up the river he saw a sight that filled him with rage. A Giantess was pouring a flood into it. This it was that was making the river rise and seethe. Thor pulled a rock out of the bank and hurled it at her. It struck her and flung her into the flood. Then she struggled out of the water and went yelping away. This Giantess was Gialp, Gerriöd's ugly and evil daughter.

Nothing would do the young Giant whom Thor had helped across but that the pair would go and visit Grid, his mother, who lived in a cave in the hillside. Loki would not go and was angered to hear that Thor thought of going. But Thor, seeing that the Giant youth was friendly, was willing enough to go to Grid's dwelling.

"Go then, but get soon to Gerriöd's dwelling yonder. I will wait for you there," said Loki. He watched Thor go up the hillside to Grid's cave. He waited until he saw Thor come back down the hillside and go toward Gerriöd's dwelling. He watched Thor go into the house where, as he thought, death awaited him. Then in a madness for what he had done, Loki, with his head drawn down on his shoulders, started running like a bird along the ground.

Grid, the old Giantess, was seated on the floor of the cave grinding corn between two stones. "Who is it?" she said, as her son led Thor within. "One of the Æsir! What Giant do you go to injure now, Asa Thor?"

"I go to injure no Giant, old Grid," Thor replied. "Look upon me! Cannot you see that I have not Miölnir, my mighty hammer, with me, nor my belt, nor my gloves of iron?"

"But where in Jötunheim do you go?"

"To the house of a friendly Giant, old Grid—to the house of Gerriöd."

"Gerriöd a friendly Giant! You are out of your wits, Asa Thor. Is he not out of his wits, my son—this one who saved you from the flood, as you say?"

"Tell him of Gerriöd, old mother," said the Giant youth.

"Do not go to his house, Asa Thor. Do not go to his house."

"My word has been given, and I should be a craven if I stayed away now, just because an old crone sitting at a quern-stone tells me I am going into a trap."

"I will give you something that will help you, Asa Thor. Lucky for you I am mistress of magical things. Take this staff in your hands. It is a staff of power and will stand you instead of Miölnir."

"I will take it since you offer it in kindness, old dame, this worm-eaten staff."

"And take these mittens, too. They will serve you for your gauntlets of iron."

"I will take them since you offer them in kindness, old dame, these worn old mittens."

"And take this length of string. It will serve you for your belt of prowess."

"I will take it since you offer it in kindness, old dame, this ragged length of string."

"'Tis well indeed for you, Asa Thor, that I am mistress of magical things."

Thor put the worn length of string around his waist, and as he did he knew that Grid, the old Giantess, was indeed the mistress of magical things. For immediately he felt his strength augmented as when he put on his own belt of strength. He then drew on the mittens and took the staff that she gave him in his hands.

He left the cave of Grid, the old Giantess, and went to Gerriöd's dwelling. Loki was not there. It was then that Thor began to think that perhaps old Grid was right and that a trap was being laid for him.

No one was in the hall. He came out of the hall and into a great stone chamber and he saw no one there either. But in the center of the stone chamber there was a stone seat, and Thor went to it and seated himself upon it.

No sooner was he seated than the chair flew upwards. Thor would have been crushed against the stone roof only that he held his staff up. So great was the power in the staff, so great was the strength that the string around him gave, that the chair was thrust downward. The stone chair crashed down upon the stone floor.

There were horrible screams from under it. Thor lifted up the seat and saw two ugly, broken bodies there. The Giant's daughters, Gialp and Greip, had hidden themselves under the chair to watch his death. But the stone that was to have crushed him against the ceiling had crushed them against the floor.

Thor strode out of that chamber with his teeth set hard. A great fire was blazing in the hall, and standing beside that fire he saw Gerriöd, the long-armed Giant.

He held a tongs into the fire. As Thor came toward him he lifted up the tongs and flung from it a blazing wedge of iron. It whizzed straight toward Thor's forehead. Thor put up his hands and caught the blazing wedge of iron between the mittens that old Grid had given him. Quickly he hurled it back at Gerriöd. It struck the Giant on the forehead and went blazing through him.

Gerriöd crashed down into the fire, and the burning iron made a blaze all around him. And when Thor reached Grid's cave (he went there to restore to the old Giantess the string, the mittens, and the staff of power she had given him) he saw the Giant's dwelling in such a blaze that one would think the fires of Muspelheim were all around it.

LOKI AGAINST THE ÆSIR

The Æsir were the guests of the Vanir: in Frey's palace the Dwellers in Asgard met and feasted in friendship. Odin and Tyr were there, Vidar and Vali, Niörd, Frey, Heimdall, and Bragi. The Asyniur and the Vana were also—Frigga, Freya, Iduna, Gerda, Skadi, Sif, and Nanna. Thor and Loki were not at the feast, for they had left Asgard together.

In Frey's palace the vessels were of shining gold; they made light for the table and they moved of their own accord to serve those who were feasting. All was peace and friendship there until Loki entered the feast hall.

Frey, smiling a welcome, showed a bench to Loki. It was beside Bragi's and next to Freya's. Loki did not take the place; instead he shouted out, "Not beside Bragi will I sit; not beside Bragi, the most craven of all the Dwellers in Asgard."

Bragi sprang up at that affront, but his wife, the mild Iduna, quieted his anger. Freya turned to Loki and reproved him for speaking injurious words at a feast.

"Freya," said Loki, "why were you not so mild when Odur was with you? Would it not have been well to have been wifely with your husband instead of breaking faith with him for the sake of a necklace that you craved of the Giant women?"

Amazement fell on all at the bitterness that was in Loki's words and looks. Tyr and Niörd stood up from their seats. But then the voice of Odin was heard and all was still for the words of the All-Father.

"Take the place beside Vidar, my silent son, O Loki," said Odin, "and let thy tongue which drips bitterness be silent."

"All the Æsir and the Vanir listen to thy words, O Odin, as if thou wert always wise and just," Loki said. "But must we forget that thou didst bring war into the world when thou didst fling thy spear at the envoys of the Vanir? And didst thou not permit me to work craftily on the one who built the wall around Asgard for a price? Thou dost speak, O Odin, and all the Æsir and the Vanir listen to thee! But was it not thou who, thinking not of wisdom but of gold when a ransom had to be made, brought the witch Gulveig out of the cave where she stayed with the Dwarf's treasure? Thou wert not always wise nor always just, O Odin, and we at the table here need not listen to thee as if always thou wert."

Then Skadi, the wife of Niörd, flung words at Loki. She spoke with all the fierceness of her Giant blood. "Why should we not rise up and chase from the hall this chattering crow?" she said.

"Skadi," said Loki, "remember that the ransom for thy father's death has not yet been paid. Thou wert glad to snatch a husband instead of it. Remember who it was that killed thy Giant father. It was I, Loki. And no ransom have I paid thee for it, although thou hast come amongst us in Asgard."

Then Loki fixed his eyes on Frey, the giver of the feast, and all knew that with bitter words he was about to assail him. But Tyr, the brave swordsman, rose up and said, "Not against Frey mayst thou speak, O Loki. Frey is generous; he is the one amongst us who spares the vanquished and frees the captive."

"Cease speaking, Tyr," said Loki. "Thou mayst not always have a hand to hold that sword of thine. Remember this saying of mine in days to come.

"Frey," said he, "because thou art the giver of the feast they think I will not speak the truth about thee. But I am not to be bribed by a feast. Didst thou not send Skirnir to Gymer's dwelling to befool Gymer's flighty daughter? Didst thou not bribe him into frightening her into a marriage with thee, who, men say, wert the slayer of her brother? Yea, Frey. Thou didst part with a charge, with the magic sword that thou shouldst have kept for the battle. Thou hadst cause to grieve when thou didst meet Beli by the lake."

When he said this all who were there of the Vanir rose up, their faces threatening Loki.

"Sit still, ye Vanir," Loki railed. "If the Æsir are to bear the brunt of Jötunheim's and Muspelheim's war upon Asgard it was your part to be the first or the last on Vigard's plain. But already ye have lost the battle for Asgard, for the weapon that was put into Frey's hands he bartered for Gerda the Giantess. Ha! Surtur shall triumph over you because of Frey's bewitchment."

In horror they looked at the one who could let his hatred speak of Surtur's triumph. All would have laid hands on Loki only Odin's voice rang out. Then another appeared at the entrance of the feasting hall. It was Thor. With his hammer upon his shoulder, his gloves of iron on his hands, and his belt of prowess around him, he stood marking Loki with wrathful eyes.

"Ha, Loki, betrayer," he shouted. "Thou didst plan to leave me dead in Gerriöd's house, but now thou wilt meet death by the stroke of this hammer."

His hands were raised to hurl Miölnir. But the words that Odin spoke were heard. "Not in this hall may slaying be done, son Thor. Keep thy hands upon thy hammer."

Then shrinking from the wrath in the eyes of Thor, Loki passed out of the feast hall. He went beyond the walls of Asgard and crossed Bifröst, the Rainbow Bridge. And he cursed Bifröst, and longed to see the day when the armies of Muspelheim would break it down in their rush against Asgard.

East of Midgard there was a place more evil than any region in Jötunheim. It was Jarnvid, the Iron Wood. There dwelt witches who were the most foul of all witches. And they had a queen over them, a hag, mother of many sons who took upon themselves the shapes of wolves. Two of her sons were Skoll and Hati, who pursued Sol, the Sun, and Mani, the Moon. She had a third son, who was Managarm, the wolf who was to be filled with the life-blood of men, who was to swallow up the Moon, and stain the heavens and earth with blood. To Jarnvid, the Iron Wood, Loki made his way. And he wed one of the witches there, Angerboda, and they had children that took on dread shapes. Loki's offspring were the most terrible of the foes that were to come against the Æsir and the Vanir in the time that was called the Twilight of the Gods.

THE CHILDREN OF LOKI

The children of Loki and the witch Angerboda were not as the children of men: they were formless as water, or air, or fire is formless, but it was given to each of them to take on the form that was most like to their own greed.

Now the Dwellers in Asgard knew that these powers of evil had been born into the world and they thought it well that they should take on forms and appear before them in Asgard. So they sent one to Jarnvid, the Iron Wood, bidding Loki bring before the Gods the powers born of him and the witch Angerboda. So Loki came into Asgard once more. And his offspring took on forms and showed themselves to the Gods. The first, whose greed was destruction, showed himself as a fearful Wolf. Fenrir he was named. And the second, whose greed was slow destruction, showed itself as a Serpent. Jörmungand it was called. The third, whose greed was for withering of all life, took on a form also. When the Gods saw it they were affrighted. For this had the form of a woman, and one side of her was that of a living woman and the other side of her was that of a corpse. Fear ran through Asgard as this form was revealed and as the name that went with it, Hela, was uttered.

Far out of sight of the Gods Hela was thrust. Odin took her and hurled her down to the deeps that are below the world. He cast her down to Niflheim, where she took to herself power over the nine regions. There, in the place that is lowest of all, Hela reigns. Her hall is Elvidnir; it is set round with high walls and it has barred gates; Precipice is the threshold of that hall; Hunger is the table within it; Care is the bed, and Burning Anguish is the hanging of the chamber.

Thor laid hold upon Jörmungand. He flung the serpent into the ocean that engirdles the world. But in the depths of the ocean Jörmungand flourished. It grew and grew until it encircled the whole world. And men knew it as the Midgard Serpent.

Fenrir the Wolf might not be seized upon by any of the Æsir. Fearfully he ranged through Asgard and they were only able to bring him to the outer courts by promising to give him all the food he was able to eat.

The Æsir shrank from feeding Fenrir. But Tyr, the brave swordsman, was willing to bring food to the Wolf's lair. Every day he brought him huge provision and fed him with the point of his sword. The Wolf grew and grew until he became monstrous and a terror in the minds of the Dwellers in Asgard.

At last the Gods in council considered it and decided that Fenrir must be bound. The chain that they would bind him with was called Laeding. In their own smithy the Gods made it and its weight was greater than Thor's hammer.

Not by force could the Gods get the fetter upon Fenrir, so they sent Skirnir, the servant of Frey, to beguile the Wolf into letting it go upon him. Skirnir came to his lair and stood near him, and he was dwarfed by the Wolf's monstrous size.

"How great may thy strength be, Mighty One?" Skirnir

asked. "Couldst thou break this chain easily? The Gods would try thee."

In scorn Fenrir looked down on the fetter Skirnir dragged. In scorn he stood still allowing Laeding to be placed upon him. Then, with an effort that was the least part of his strength, he stretched himself and broke the chain in two.

The Gods were dismayed. But they took more iron, and with greater fires and mightier hammer blows they forged another fetter. Dromi, this one was called, and it was half again as strong as Laeding was. Skirnir the Venturesome brought it to the Wolf's lair, and in scorn Fenrir let the mightier chain be placed upon him.

He shook himself and the chain held. Then his eyes became fiery and he stretched himself with a growl and a snarl. Dromi broke across, and Fenrir stood looking balefully at Skirnir.

The Gods saw that no chain they could forge would bind Fenrir and they fell more and more into fear of him. They took council again and they bethought them of the wonder-work the Dwarfs had made for them, the spear Gungnir, the ship Skidbladnir, the hammer Miölnir. Could the Dwarfs be got to make the fetter to bind Fenrir? If they would do it the Gods would add to their domain.

Skirnir went down to Svartheim with the message from Asgard. The Dwarf Chief swelled with pride to think that it was left to them to make the fetter that would bind Fenrir.

"We Dwarfs can make a fetter that will bind the Wolf," he said. "Out of six things we will make it."

"What are these six things?" Skirnir asked.

"The roots of stones, the breath of a fish, the beards of women, the noise made by the footfalls of cats, the sinews of bears, the spittle of a bird."

"I have never heard the noise made by a cat's footfall, nor

have I seen the roots of stones nor the beards of women. But use what things you will, O Helper of the Gods."

The Chief brought his six things together and the Dwarfs in their smithy worked for days and nights. They forged a fetter that was named Gleipnir. Smooth and soft as a silken string it was. Skirnir brought it to Asgard and put it into the hands of the Gods.

Then a day came when the Gods said that once again they should try to put a fetter upon Fenrir. But if he was to be bound they would bind him far from Asgard. Lyngvi was an island that they often went to to make sport, and they spoke of going there. Fenrir growled that he would go with them. He came and he sported in his own terrible way. And then as if it were to make more sport, one of the Æsir shook out the smooth cord and showed it to Fenrir.

"It is stronger than you might think, Mighty One," they said. "Will you not let it go upon you that we may see you break it?"

Fenrir out of his fiery eyes looked scorn upon them. "What fame would there be for me," he said, "in breaking such a binding?"

They showed him that none in their company could break it, slender as it was. "Thou only art able to break it, Mighty One," they said.

"The cord is slender, but there may be an enchantment in it," Fenrir said.

"Thou canst not break it, Fenrir, and we need not dread thee any more," the Gods said.

Then was the Wolf ravenous wroth, for he lived on the fear that he made in the minds of the Gods. "I am loth to have this binding upon me," he said, "but if one of the Æsir will put his hand in my mouth as a pledge that I shall be freed of it, I will let ye put it on me."

The Gods looked wistfully on one another. It would be health to them all to have Fenrir bound, but who would lose his hand to have it done? One and then another of the Æsir stepped backward. But not Tyr, the brave swordsman. He stepped to Fenrir and laid his left hand before those tremendous jaws.

"Not thy left hand—thy swordhand, O Tyr," growled Fenrir, and Tyr put his swordhand into that terrible mouth.

Then the cord Gleipnir was put upon Fenrir. With fiery eyes he watched the Gods bind him. When the binding was on him he stretched himself as before. He stretched himself to a monstrous size but the binding did not break off him. Then with fury he snapped his jaws upon the hand, and Tyr's hand, the swordsman's hand, was torn off.

But Fenrir was bound. They fixed a mighty chain to the fetter, and they passed the chain through a hole they bored through a great rock. The monstrous Wolf made terrible efforts to break loose, but the rock and the chain and the fetter held. Then seeing him secured, and to avenge the loss of Tyr's hand, the Gods took Tyr's sword and drove it to the hilt through his underjaw. Horribly the Wolf howled. Mightily the foam flowed down from his jaws. That foam flowing made a river that is called Von—a river of fury that flowed on until Ragnarök came, the Twilight of the Gods.

BALDUR'S DOOM

In Asgard there were two places that meant strength and joy to the Æsir and the Vanir: one was the garden where grew the apples that Iduna gathered, and the other was the Peace Stead, where, in a palace called Breidablik, Baldur the Well-Beloved dwelt.

In the Peace Stead no crime had ever been committed, no blood had ever been shed, no falseness had ever been spoken. Contentment came into the minds of all in Asgard when they thought upon this place. Ah! Were it not that the Peace Stead was there, happy with Baldur's presence, the minds of the Æsir and the Vanir might have become gloomy and stern from thinking on the direful things that were arrayed against them.

Baldur was beautiful. So beautiful was he that all the white blossoms on the earth were called by his name. Baldur was happy. So happy was he that all the birds on the earth sang his name. So just and so wise was Baldur that the judgment he pronounced might never be altered. Nothing foul or unclean had ever come near where he had his dwelling:

'Tis Breidablik called,
Where Baldur the Fair
Hath built him a bower,
In the land where I know
Least loathliness lies.

HEALING THINGS WERE DONE in Baldur's Stead. Tyr's wrist was healed of the wounds that Fenrir's fangs had made. And there Frey's mind became less troubled with the foreboding that Loki had filled it with when he railed at him about the bartering of his sword.

Now after Fenrir had been bound to the rock in the faraway island the Æsir and the Vanir knew a while of contentment. They passed bright days in Baldur's Stead, listening to the birds that made music there. And it was there that Bragi the Poet wove into his never-ending story the tale of Thor's adventures amongst the Giants.

But even into Baldur's Stead foreboding came. One day little Hnossa, the child of Freya and the lost Odur, was brought there in such sorrow that no one outside could comfort her. Nanna, Baldur's gentle wife, took the child upon her lap and found ways of soothing her. Then Hnossa told of a dream that had filled her with fright.

She had dreamt of Hela, the Queen that is half living woman and half corpse. In her dream Hela had come into Asgard saying, "A lord of the Æsir I must have to dwell with me in my realm beneath the earth." Hnossa had such fear from this dream that she had fallen into a deep sorrow.

A silence fell upon all when the dream of Hnossa was told. Nanna looked wistfully at Odin All-Father. And Odin, looking at Frigga, saw that a fear had entered her breast.

He left the Peace Stead and went to his watchtower Hlidskjalf. He waited there till Hugin and Munin should come to him.

Every day his two ravens flew through the world, and coming back to him told him of all that was happening. And now they might tell him of happenings that would let him guess if Hela had indeed turned her thoughts toward Asgard, or if she had the power to draw one down to her dismal abode.

The ravens flew to him, and lighting one on each of his shoulders, told him of things that were being said up and down Ygdrassil, the World Tree. Ratatösk the Squirrel was saying them. And Ratatösk had heard them from the brood of serpents that with Nidhögg, the great dragon, gnawed ever at the root of Ygdrassil. He told it to the Eagle that sat ever on the topmost bough, that in Hela's habitation a bed was spread and a chair was left empty for some lordly comer.

And hearing this, Odin thought that it were better that Fenrir the Wolf should range ravenously through Asgard than that Hela should win one from amongst them to fill that chair and lie in that bed.

He mounted Sleipner, his eight-legged steed, and rode down toward the abodes of the Dead. For three days and three nights of silence and darkness he journeyed on. Once one of the hounds of Helheim broke loose and bayed upon Sleipner's tracks. For a day and a night Garm, the hound, pursued them, and Odin smelled the blood that dripped from his monstrous jaws.

At last he came to where, wrapped in their shrouds, a field of the Dead lay. He dismounted from Sleipner and called upon one to rise and speak with him. It was on Volva, a dead prophetess, he called. And when he pronounced her name he uttered a rune that had the power to break the sleep of the Dead.

There was a groaning in the middle of where the shrouded ones lay. Then Odin cried, out, "Arise, Volva, prophetess." There was a stir in the middle of where the shrouded ones lay, and a head and shoulders were thrust up from amongst the Dead.

"Who calls on Volva the Prophetess? The rains have drenched my flesh and the storms have shaken my bones for more seasons than the living know. No living voice has a right to call me from my sleep with the Dead."

"It is Vegtam the Wanderer who calls. For whom is the bed prepared and the seat left empty in Hela's habitation?"

"For Baldur, Odin's son, is the bed prepared and the seat left empty. Now let me go back to my sleep with the Dead."

But now Odin saw beyond Volva's prophecy. "Who is it," he cried out, "that stands with unbowed head and that will not lament for Baldur? Answer, Volva, prophetess!"

"Thou seest far, but thou canst not see clearly. Thou art Odin. I can see clearly but I cannot see far. Now let me go back to my sleep with the Dead."

"Volva, prophetess!" Odin cried out again.

But the voice from amongst the shrouded ones said, "Thou canst not wake me any more until the fires of Muspelheim blaze above my head."

Then there was silence in the field of the Dead, and Odin turned Sleipner, his steed, and for four days, through the gloom and silence, he journeyed back to Asgard.

Frigga had felt the fear that Odin had felt. She looked toward Baldur, and the shade of Hela came between her and her son. But then she heard the birds sing in the Peace Stead and she knew that none of all the things in the world would injure Baldur.

And to make it sure she went to all the things that could hurt him and from each of them she took an oath that it would not injure Baldur, the Well-Beloved. She took an oath from fire and from water, from iron and from all metals, from earths and stones and great trees, from birds and beasts and creeping things, from poisons and diseases. Very readily they all gave the oath that they would work no injury on Baldur.

Then when Frigga went back and told what she had accomplished the gloom that had lain on Asgard lifted. Baldur would be spared to them. Hela might have a place prepared in her dark habitation, but neither fire nor water, nor iron nor any metals, nor earths nor stones nor great woods, nor birds nor beasts nor creeping things, nor poisons nor diseases, would help her to bring him down. "Hela has no arms to draw you to her," the Æsir and the Vanir cried to Baldur.

Hope was renewed for them and they made games to honor Baldur. They had him stand in the Peace Stead and they brought against him all the things that had sworn to leave him hurtless. And neither the battle-axe flung full at him, nor the stone out of the sling, nor the burning brand, nor the deluge of water would injure the beloved of Asgard. The Æsir and the Vanir laughed joyously to see these things fall harmlessly from him while a throng came to join them in the games; Dwarfs and friendly Giants.

But Loki the Hater came in with that throng. He watched the games from afar. He saw the missiles and the weapons being flung and he saw Baldur stand smiling and happy under the strokes of metal and stones and great woods. He wondered at the sight, but he knew that he might not ask the meaning of it from the ones who knew him.

He changed his shape into that of an old woman and he went amongst those who were making sport for Baldur. He spoke to Dwarfs and friendly Giants. "Go to Frigga and ask. Go to Frigga and ask," was all the answer Loki got from any of them.

Then to Fensalir, Frigga's mansion, Loki went. He told those in the mansion that he was Groa, the old Enchantress who was drawing out of Thor's head the fragments of a grindstone that a Giant's throw had embedded in it. Frigga knew about Groa and she praised the Enchantress for what she had done.

"Many fragments of the great grindstone have I taken out of Thor's head by the charms I know," said the pretended Groa. "Thor was so grateful that he brought back to me the husband that he once had carried off to the end of the earth. So overjoyed was I to find my husband restored that I forgot the rest of the charms. And I left some fragments of the stone in Thor's head."

So Loki said, repeating a story that was true. "Now I remember the rest of the charm," he said, "and I can draw out the fragments of the stone that are left. But will you not tell me, O Queen, what is the meaning of the extraordinary things I saw the Æsir and the Vanir doing?"

"I will tell you," said Frigga, looking kindly and happily at the pretended old woman. "They are hurling all manner of heavy and dangerous things at Baldur, my beloved son. And all Asgard cheers to see that neither metal nor stone nor great wood will hurt him."

"But why will they not hurt him?" said the pretended Enchantress.

"Because I have drawn an oath from all dangerous and threatening things to leave Baldur hurtless," said Frigga.

"From all things, lady? Is there no thing in all the world that has not taken an oath to leave Baldur hurtless?"

"Well, indeed, there is one thing that has not taken the oath. But that thing is so small and weak that I passed it by without taking thought of it."

"What can it be, lady?"

"The Mistletoe that is without root or strength. It grows on the eastern side of Valhalla. I passed it by without drawing an oath from it."

"Surely you were not wrong to pass it by. What could the Mistletoe—the rootless Mistletoe—do against Baldur?"

Saying this the pretended Enchantress hobbled off.

But not far did the pretender go hobbling. He changed his gait and hurried to the eastern side of Valhalla. There a great oak tree flourished and out of a branch of it a little bush of Mistletoe grew. Loki broke off a spray and with it in his hand he went to where the Æsir and the Vanir were still playing games to honor Baldur.

All were laughing as Loki drew near, for the Giants and the Dwarfs, the Asyniur and the Vana, were all casting missiles. The Giants threw too far and the Dwarfs could not throw far enough, while the Asyniur and the Vana threw far and wide of the mark. In the midst of all that glee and gamesomeness it was strange to see one standing joyless. But one stood so, and he was of the Æsir—Hödur, Baldur's blind brother.

"Why do you not enter the game?" said Loki to him in his changed voice.

"I have no missile to throw at Baldur," Hödur said.

"Take this and throw it," said Loki. "It is a twig of the Mistletoe."

"I cannot see to throw it," said Hödur.

"I will guide your hand," said Loki. He put the twig of Mistletoe in Hödur's hand and he guided the hand for the throw. The twig flew toward Baldur. It struck him on the breast and it pierced him. Then Baldur fell down with a deep groan.

The Æsir and the Vanir, the Dwarfs and the friendly Giants, stood still in doubt and fear and amazement. Loki slipped away. And blind Hödur, from whose hand the twig of Mistletoe had gone, stood quiet, not knowing that his throw had bereft Baldur of life.

Then a wailing rose around the Peace Stead. It was from the Asyniur and the Vana. Baldur was dead, and they began to lament him. And while they were lamenting him, the beloved of Asgard, Odin came amongst them.

"Hela has won our Baldur from us," Odin said to Frigga as they both bent over the body of their beloved son.

"Nay, I will not say it," Frigga said.

When the Æsir and the Vanir had won their senses back the mother of Baldur went amongst them. "Who amongst you would win my love and goodwill?" she said. "Whoever would let him ride down to Hela's dark realm and ask the Queen to take ransom for Baldur. It may be she will take it and let Baldur come back to us. Who amongst you will go? Odin's steed is ready for the journey."

Then forth stepped Hermod the Nimble, the brother of Baldur. He mounted Sleipner and turned the eight-legged steed down toward Hela's dark realm.

For nine days and nine nights Hermod rode on. His way was through rugged glens, one deeper and darker than the other. He came to the river that is called Giöll and to the bridge across it that is all glittering with gold. The pale maid who guards the bridge spoke to him.

"The hue of life is still on thee," said Modgudur, the pale maid. "Why dost thou journey down to Hela's deathly realm?"

"I am Hermod," he said, "and I go to see if Hela will take ransom for Baldur."

"Fearful is Hela's habitation for one to come to," said Modgudur, the pale maid. "All round it is a steep wall that even thy steed might hardly leap. Its threshold is Precipice. The bed therein is Care, the table is Hunger, the hanging of the chamber is Burning Anguish."

"It may be that Hela will take ransom for Baldur."

"If all things in the world still lament for Baldur, Hela will have to take ransom and let him go from her," said Modgudur, the pale maid that guards the glittering bridge.

"It is well, then, for all things lament Baldur. I will go to her and make her take ransom."

"Thou mayst not pass until it is of a surety that all things still lament him. Go back to the world and make sure. If thou dost come to this glittering bridge and tell me that all things still lament Baldur, I will let thee pass and Hela will have to hearken to thee."

"I will come back to thee, and thou, Modgudur, pale maid, wilt have to let me pass."

"Then I will let thee pass," said Modgudur.

Joyously Hermod turned Sleipner and rode back through the rugged glens, each one less gloomy than the other. He reached the upper world, and saw that all things were still lamenting for Baldur. Joyously Hermod rode onward. He met the Vanir in the middle of the world and he told them the happy tidings.

Then Hermod and the Vanir went through the world seeking out each thing and finding that each thing still wept for Baldur. But one day Hermod came upon a crow that was sitting on the dead branch of a tree. The crow made no lament as he came near. She rose up and flew away and Hermod followed her to make sure that she lamented for Baldur.

He lost sight of her near a cave. And then before the cave he saw a hag with blackened teeth who raised no voice of lament.

"If thou art the crow that came flying here, make lament for Baldur," Hermod said.

"I, Thaukt, will make no lament for Baldur," the hag said, "let Hela keep what she holds."

"All things weep tears for Baldur," Hermod said.

"I will weep dry tears for him," said the hag.

She hobbled into her cave, and as Hermod followed a crow fluttered out. He knew that this was Thaukt, the evil hag, transformed. He followed her, and she went through the world croaking, "Let Hela keep what she holds. Let Hela keep what she holds."

Then Hermod knew that he might not ride to Hela's habitation. All things knew that there was one thing in the world that would not lament for Baldur. The Vanir came back to him, and with head bowed over Sleipner's mane, Hermod rode into Asgard.

Now the Æsir and the Vanir, knowing that no ransom would be taken for Baldur and that the joy and content of Asgard were gone indeed, made ready his body for the burning. First they covered Baldur's body with a rich robe, and each left beside it his most precious possession. Then they all took leave of him, kissing him upon the brow. But Nanna, his gentle wife, flung herself on his dead breast and her heart broke and she died of her grief. Then did the Æsir and the Vanir weep afresh. And they took the body of Nanna and they placed it side by side with Baldur's.

On his own great ship, Ringhorn, would Baldur be placed with Nanna beside him. Then the ship would be launched on the water and all would be burned with fire.

But it was found that none of the Æsir or the Vanir were able to launch Baldur's great ship. Hyrroken, a Giantess, was sent for. She came mounted on a great wolf with twisted serpents for a bridle. Four Giants held fast the wolf when she alighted. She came to the ship and with a single push she sent it into the sea. The rollers struck out fire as the ship dashed across them.

Then when it rode the water fires mounted on the ship. And in the blaze of the fires one was seen bending over the body of Baldur and whispering into his ear. It was Odin All-Father. Then he went down off the ship and all the fires rose into a mighty burning. Speechlessly the Æsir and the Vanir watched with tears streaming down their faces while all things lamented, crying, "Baldur the Beautiful is dead, is dead."

And what was it that Odin All-Father whispered to Baldur as he bent above him with the flames of the burning ship around? He whispered of a heaven above Asgard that Surtur's flames might not reach, and of a life that would come to beauty again after the World of Men and the World of the Gods had been searched through and through with fire.

LOKI'S PUNISHMENT

The crow went flying toward the North, croaking as she flew, "Let Hela keep what she holds. Let Hela keep what she holds." That crow was the hag Thaukt transformed, and the hag Thaukt was Loki.

He flew to the North and came into the wastes of Jötunheim. As a crow he lived there, hiding himself from the wrath of the Gods. He told the Giants that the time had come for them to build the ship Naglfar, the ship that was to be built out of the nails of dead men, and that was to sail to Asgard on the day of Ragnarök with the Giant Hrymer steering it. And harkening to what he said the Giants then and there began to build Naglfar, the ship that Gods and men wished to remain unbuilt for long.

Then Loki, tiring of the wastes of Jötunheim, flew to the burning South. As a lizard he lived amongst the rocks of Muspelheim, and he made the Fire Giants rejoice when he told them of the loss of Frey's sword and of Tyr's right hand.

But still in Asgard there was one who wept for Loki—

Siguna, his wife. Although he had left her and had shown his hatred for her, Siguna wept for her evil husband.

He left Muspelheim as he had left Jötunheim and he came to live in the World of Men. He knew that he had now come into a place where the wrath of the Gods might find him, and so he made plans to be ever ready for escape. He had come to the River where, ages before, he had slain the otter that was the son of the Enchanter, and on the very rock where the otter had eaten the salmon on the day of his killing, Loki built his house. He made four doors to it so that he might see in every direction. And the power that he kept for himself was the power of transforming himself into a salmon.

Often as a salmon he swam in the River. But even for the fishes that swam beside him Loki had hatred. Out of flax and yarn he wove a net that men might have the means of taking them out of the water.

The wrath that the Gods had against Loki did not pass away. It was he who, as Thaukt, the Hag, had given Hela the power to keep Baldur unransomed. It was he who had put into Hödur's hand the sprig of Mistletoe that had bereft Baldur of life. Empty was Asgard now that

Baldur lived no more in the Peace Stead, and stern and gloomy grew the minds of the Æsir and the Vanir with thinking on the direful things that were arrayed against them. Odin in his hall of Valhalla thought only of the ways by which he could bring heroes to him to be his help in defending Asgard.

The Gods searched through the world and they found at last the place where Loki had made his dwelling. He was weaving the net to take fishes when he saw them coming from four directions. He threw the net into the fire so that it was burnt, and he sprang into the River and transformed himself into a salmon. When the Gods entered his dwelling they found only the burnt-out fire.

But there was one amongst them who could understand all that he saw. In the ashes were the marks of the burnt net and he knew that these were the tracing of something to catch fishes. And from the marks left in the ashes he made a net that was the same as the one Loki had burnt.

With it in their hands the Gods went down the River, dragging the net through the water. Loki was affrighted to find the thing of his own weaving brought against him. He lay between two stones at the bottom of the River, and the net passed over him.

But the Gods knew that the net had touched something at the bottom. They fastened weights to it and they dragged the net through the River again. Loki knew that he might not escape it this time and he rose in the water and swam toward the sea. The Gods caught sight of him as he leaped over a waterfall. They followed him, dragging the net. Thor waded behind, ready to seize him should he turn back.

Loki came out at the mouth of the River and behold! There was a great eagle hovering over the waves of the sea and ready to swoop down on fishes. He turned back in the River. He made a leap that took him over the net that the Gods were dragging. But Thor was behind the net and he caught the salmon in his powerful hands and he held him for all the struggle that Loki made. No fish had ever struggled so before. Loki got himself free all but his tail, but Thor held to the tail and brought him amongst the rocks and forced him to take on his proper form.

He was in the hands of those whose wrath was strong against him. They brought him to a cavern and they bound him to three sharp-pointed rocks. With cords that were made of the sinews of wolves they bound him, and they transformed the cords into iron bands. There they would have left Loki bound and helpless. But Skadi, with her fierce Giant blood, was not content that he should be left untormented. She found a serpent that had deadly venom and she hung this serpent above Loki's head. The drops of venom fell upon him, bringing him anguish drop by drop, minute by minute. So Loki's torture went on.

But Siguna with the pitying heart came to his relief. She exiled herself from Asgard, and endured the darkness and the cold of the cavern, that she might take some of the torment away from him who was her husband. Over Loki Siguna stood, holding in her hands a cup into which fell the serpent's venom, thus sparing him from the full measure of anguish. Now and then Siguna had to turn aside to spill out the flowing cup, and then the drops of venom fell upon Loki and he screamed in agony, twisting in his bonds. It was then that men felt the earth quake. There in his bonds Loki stayed until the coming of Ragnarök, the Twilight of the Gods.

THE TWILIGHT
OF THE GODS

Snow fell on the four quarters of the world; icy winds blew from every side; the sun and the moon were hidden by storms. It was the Fimbul Winter: no spring came and no summer; no autumn brought harvest or fruit, and winter grew into winter again.

There was three years' winter. The first was called the Winter of Winds: storms blew and snows drove down and frosts were mighty. The children of men might hardly keep alive in that dread winter.

The second winter was called the Winter of the Sword: those who were left alive amongst men robbed and slew for what was left to feed on; brother fell on brother and slew him, and over all the world there were mighty battles.

And the third winter was called the Winter of the Wolf. Then the ancient witch who lived in Jarnvid, the Iron Wood, fed the Wolf Managarm on unburied men and on the corpses of those who fell in battle. Mightily grew and flourished the Wolf that was to be the devourer of Mani, the Moon. The Champions in Valhalla would find their seats splashed with the blood that Managarm dashed from his jaws; this was a sign to the Gods that the time of the last battle was approaching.

A cock crew; far down in the bowels of the earth he was and beside Hela's habitation: the rusty-red cock of Hel crew, and his crowing made a stir in the lower worlds. In Jötunheim a cock crew, Fialar, the crimson cock, and at his crowing the Giants aroused themselves. High up in Asgard a cock crew, the golden cock Gullinkambir, and at his crowing the Champions in Valhalla bestirred themselves.

A dog barked; deep down in the earth a dog barked; it was Garm, the hound with bloody mouth, barking in Gnipa's Cave. The Dwarfs who heard groaned before their doors of stone. The tree Ygdrassil moaned in all its branches. There was a rending noise as the Giants moved their ship; there was a trampling sound as the hosts of Muspelheim gathered their horses.

But Jötunheim and Muspelheim and Hel waited tremblingly; it might be that Fenrir the Wolf might not burst the bonds wherewith the Gods had bound him. Without his being loosed the Gods might not be destroyed. And then was heard the rending of the rock as Fenrir broke loose. For the second time the Hound Garm barked in Gnipa's Cave.

Then was heard the galloping of the horses of the riders of Muspelheim; then was heard the laughter of Loki; then was heard the blowing of Heimdall's horn; then was heard the opening of Valhalla's five hundred and forty doors, as eight hundred Champions made ready to pass through each door.

Odin took council with Mimir's head. Up from the waters of the Well of Wisdom he drew it, and by the power of the runes he knew he made the head speak to him. Where best might the Æsir and the Vanir and the Einherjar, who were the Champions of Midgard, meet, and how best might they strive with the forces of Muspelheim and Jötunheim and Hel? The head of Mimir counseled Odin to meet them on Vigard Plain and to wage there such war that the powers of evil would be destroyed forever, even though his own world should be destroyed with them.

The riders of Muspelheim reached Bifröst, the Rainbow Bridge. Now would they storm the City of the Gods and fill it with flame. But Bifröst broke under the weight of the riders of Muspelheim, and they came not to the City of the Gods.

Jörmungand, the serpent that encircles the world, reared itself up from the sea. The waters flooded the lands, and the remnant of the world's inhabitants was swept away. That mighty flood floated Naglfar, the Ship of Nails that the Giants were so long building, and floated the ship of Hel also. With Hrymer the Giant steering it, Naglfar sailed against the Gods, with all the powers of Jötunheim aboard. And Loki steered the ship of Hel with the Wolf Fenrir upon it for the place of the last battle.

Since Bifröst was broken, the Æsir and the Vanir, the Asyniur and the Vana, the Einherjar and the Valkyries rode downward to Vigard through the waters of Thund. Odin rode at the head of his Champions. His helmet was of gold and in his hand was his spear Gungnir. Thor and Tyr were in his company.

In Mirkvid, the Dark Forest, the Vanir stood against the host of Muspelheim. From the broken end of the Rainbow Bridge the riders came, all flashing and flaming, with fire before them and after them. Niörd was there with Skadi, his Giant wife, fierce in her war-dress; Freya was there also, and Frey had Gerda beside him as a battle-maiden. Terribly bright flashed Surtur's sword. No sword ever owned was as bright as his except the sword that Frey had given to Skirnir. Frey and Surtur fought; he perished, Frey perished in that battle, but he would not have perished if he had had in his hand his own magic sword.

And now, for the third time, Garm, the hound with blood upon his jaws, barked. He had broken loose on the world, and with fierce bounds he rushed toward Vigard Plain, where the Gods had assembled their powers. Loud barked Garm. The Eagle Hræsvelgur screamed on the edge of heaven. Then the skies were cloven, and the tree Ygdrassil was shaken in all its roots.

To the place where the Gods had drawn up their ranks came the ship of Jötunheim and the ship of Hel, came the riders of Muspelheim, and Garm, the hound with blood upon his jaws. And out of the sea that now surrounded the plain of Vigard the serpent Jörmungand came.

What said Odin to the Gods and to the Champions who surrounded him? "We will give our lives and let our world be destroyed, but we will battle so that these evil powers will not live after us." Out of Hel's ship sprang Fenrir the Wolf. His mouth gaped; his lower jaw hung against the earth, and his upper jaw scraped the sky. Against the Wolf Odin All-Father fought. Thor might not aid him, for Thor had now to encounter Jörmungand, the monstrous serpent.

By Fenrir the Wolf Odin was slain. But the younger Gods were now advancing to the battle; and Vidar, the Silent God, came face to face with Fenrir. He laid his foot on the Wolf's lower jaw, that foot that had on the sandal made of all the scraps of leather that shoemakers had laid by for him, and with his hands he seized the upper jaw and tore his gullet. Thus died Fenrir, the fiercest of all the enemies of the Gods.

Jörmungand, the monstrous serpent, would have overwhelmed all with the venom he was ready to pour forth. But Thor sprang forward and crushed him with a stroke of his hammer Miölnir. Then Thor stepped back nine paces. But the serpent blew his venom over him, and blinded and choked and burnt, Thor, the World's Defender, perished.

Loki sprang from his ship and strove with Heimdall, the Warder of the Rainbow Bridge and the Watcher for the Gods. Loki slew Heimdall and was slain by him.

Bravely fought Tyr, the God who had sacrificed his sword-hand for the binding of the Wolf. Bravely he fought, and many of the powers of evil perished by his strong left hand. But Garm, the hound with bloody jaws, slew Tyr.

And now the riders of Muspelheim came down on the field. Bright and gleaming were all their weapons. Before them and behind them went wasting fires. Surtur cast fire upon the earth; the tree Ygdrassil took fire and burned in all its great branches; the World Tree was wasted in the blaze. But the fearful fire that Surtur brought on the earth destroyed him and all his host.

The Wolf Hati caught up on Sol, the Sun; the Wolf Managarm seized on Mani, the Moon; they devoured them; stars fell, and darkness came down on the world.

The seas flowed over the burnt and wasted earth and the skies were dark above the sea, for Sol and Mani were no more. But at last the seas drew back and earth appeared again, green and beautiful. A new Sun and a new Moon appeared in the heavens, one a daughter of Sol and the other a daughter of Mani. No grim wolves kept them in pursuit.

Four of the younger Gods stood on the highest of the world's peaks; they were Vidar and Vali, the sons of Odin, and Modi and Magni, the sons of Thor. Modi and Magni found Miölnir, Thor's hammer, and with it they slew the monsters that still raged through the world, the Hound Garm and the Wolf Managarm.

Vidar and Vali found in the grass the golden tablets on which were inscribed the runes of wisdom of the elder Gods.

The runes told them of a heaven that was above Asgard, of Gimli, that was untouched by Surtur's fire. Vili and Ve, Will and Holiness, ruled in it. Baldur and Hödur came from Hela's habitation, and the Gods sat on the peak together and held speech with each other, calling to mind the secrets and the happenings they had known before Ragnarök, the Twilight of the Gods.

Deep in a wood two of human kind were left; the fire of Surtur did not touch them; they slept, and when they wakened the world was green and beautiful again. These two fed on the dews of the morning; a woman and a man they were. Lif and Lifthrasir. They walked abroad in the world, and from them and from their children came the men and women who spread themselves over the earth.

The End.

PUBLISHER'S NOTE

This book was produced as part of the Publishing master's degree program at Western Colorado University, Graduate Program in Creative Writing. The students worked cooperatively to produce these fine new editions of worthy public-domain works. The intent is to bring literary classics to a new readership. For the enjoyment of a modern audience, some minor revisions to archaic terms or punctuation may have been made.

Because these works were written in a different time, some attitudes and phrasing may seem outdated to a modern audience. After careful consideration, rather than revising the author's work, we have chosen to preserve the original wording and intent.

ABOUT THE AUTHOR

Padraic Colum is a Newbery honor winning author, famous for collecting folklore from around the world and for being a significant part of the Irish Literary Revival in the early 20th century.

He was born in Ireland, the oldest of eight children, and moved to the United States in his later youth. There, he created collections of children's stories honoring various heritages across Europe. Some of his works include *The King of Ireland's Sons, The Adventures of Odyseuss, The Castle Conquest*, and *The Flying Swans*. Three of his children's books have been awarded the Newbery Honor Prize and a first edition copy of *At The Gateways of the Day* was gifted to President Barack Obama.

He also wrote poems, plays, and created the screenplay for an animated film. His plays helped found the famous Abbey Theater, one of the country's biggest cultural centers. Some of his plays include *The Saxon Shilling, Mogue the Wanderer, Broken Sail*, and *The Land*. Additionally, he compiled Irish folk songs and adapted them.

Thanks to the efforts of Padraic Colum, a rich heritage of International lore has been preserved and shared throughout the world.

ABOUT THE EDITOR

Amy Michelle Carpenter is a bestselling, award-winning author of young adult science fiction. She is the owner of Monster Ivy Publishing, a publisher of edgy, clean fiction with over thirty titles, including The Kiss List, which is currently being filmed as a movie by MarVista. Other titles include Readers Favorite winners and Whitney Award finalists, as well as several international bestsellers.

She is a professional developmental editor. She has edited and written hundreds of blogs and articles for various national and local outlets including *The Voice of Scouting, The Boy Scout, The Herald Journal,* and *The Universe.* In addition, she has presented at Utah Valley University Writers Academy, LTUE, and Quills Conference on editing and character development.

Her current efforts include working towards a masters in publishing under *New York Times* bestselling author Kevin J. Anderson as well as doing editing work for *Gilded Glass,* an anthology by executive editors Kevin J. Anderson and Allyson

WORDFIRE CLASSICS

The Lost World
The Poison Belt
by A. Conan Doyle

The Wolf Leader
by Alexandre Dumas

The Cthulhu Stories of Robert E. Howard
by Robert E. Howard

The Detective Stories of Edgar Allan Poe
by Edgar Allan Poe

The Jewel of Seven Stars (Annotated)
by Bram Stoker

From the Earth to the Moon and Around the Moon
by Jules Verne

The Complete War of the Worlds
The War in the Air
Kipps: The Story of a Simple Man
The Sleeper Awakes and Men Like Gods
by H.G. Wells

*Mother of Frankenstein: Maria: or, The Wrongs of Woman &
Memoirs of the Author of A Vindication of the Rights of Woman*
by Mary Wollstonecraft

We: The 100th Anniversary Edition
by Yevgeny Zamyatin

*One Stormy Night : A Story Challenge That Created the Gothic
Horror Genre*
by Lord Byron, Dr. John William Polidori, and Mary Shelley

HOLIDAY CLASSICS
The Ghost of Christmas Always
by Charles Dickens & Kevin J. Anderson

The Santa Claus Stories
by L. Frank Baum

Our list of other WordFire Press authors and titles is always
growing. To find out more and to shop our selection of titles,
visit us at:
wordfirepress.com

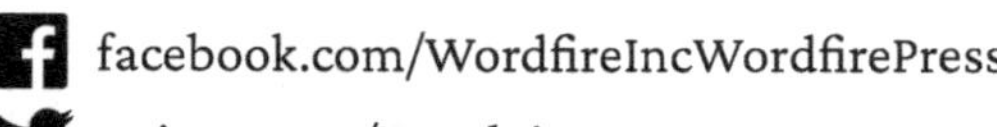

facebook.com/WordfireIncWordfirePress

twitter.com/WordFirePress

instagram.com/WordFirePress

bookbub.com/profile/4109784512